Denise Hill
The Window

Denise Hill
The Window

The Window
By
Denise Hill

Denise Hill
The Window

ACKNOWLEDMENT

Oh my God! Book number six. All the glory goes to God for allowing me the opportunity to tell my stories. I have such a wild imagination that I express through my writing.

I want to thank those that support me and the ones who don't. When you have people that you know, friends or even family members that don't support you, it can be unsettling, sometimes, but I say keep doing what you're doing, never give up just because some people don't support you. The only support you need is from God!

I want to thank my son Daniel and daughter Devin, who are my biggest supporters. Thanks for the encouragement because without you guys, I don't know where I would be today.

The window came to me in a dream. I had a dream that I witnessed a murder while looking out a window, so I decided to turn it into a book. I would love to see this as a weekly television series, so I might do something a little different with a weekly audio series. I hope you guys enjoy this book as much as I enjoyed writing. Thanks and God bless!

Denise Hill
The Window

DH PUBLISHING COMPANY
PO BOX 333
INDIANAPOLIS, IN 46250

Denise Hill
The Window

Prologue

Ronnie sat behind his desk and watched Jerome and Diamond. He knew something was going on with those two. He only hoped Jerome was smart and that he protect her. Ronnie shut the camera down when they entered the bedroom. He sat there and shook his head. He was young once, so he truly understood. He only wished he could be so lucky and get with her mother, Gina.

Music played in the background, "Ice on My Baby" by Yung Bleu as Jerome pulled Diamond to him. He kissed her softly as he lifted her shirt up and over her head. He moved down to her perky breasts and took one into his mouth as a moan escaped. He took the other nipple into his mouth until it became hard. Jerome picked her up. She wrapped her legs around his waist as he moved toward the bed. Jerome laid her down and pulled her pajama pants off and pulled her closer to the edge of the bed. He looked down at her.

"Are you ready for me?"

Diamond was afraid, and she didn't know what to expect since it was her first time.

Diamond whispered, "I guess so."

"Don't worry. I will be gentle with you," Jerome promised.

Jerome removed his boxers as Diamond laid there admiring him. Seconds later, Jerome slid the tip in.

"No! Oh my God, get up!" Diamond said as she tried to scoot up, but Jerome pulled her back.

"It's just the head. The pain won't last long, I promise."

Jerome moved slowly in and out, deeper and deeper.

Minutes later, Diamond screamed, "Oh my God! Jerome!"

"Does it feel good, baby?" Jerome asked.

"Jerome, yes!" Diamond watched Jerome as he stroked her slow and then fast. Jerome looked like the Rapper Common. The first time Diamond laid eyes on Jerome, she knew she wanted him to be her first, but she didn't think it would happen so soon.

Denise Hill
The Window

CHAPTER ONE

Late fall

A low-income neighborhood, several apartment buildings, kids playing in the playground, and music playing loud as the sound of Ella Mae Boo'd up played, as four young men sat inside a late model Buick Regal getting high and drinking.

"Man, this shit is the fire," JJ said as he took another pull off the joint.

"I know, that's why everyone has been blowing my phone up. I made ten geez last week," Lil Moe said.

"No shit! Man, you got to put me on, I want to make some money too."

"You know what you have to do," Ricky said as he handed the joint to Harry.

"Hell yeah! It's initiation time!" JJ yelled.

Gina was in the kitchen preparing dinner. She lifted the top up and checked on the brown rice that was cooking. She stirred the vegetables and added some sliced grilled chicken.

"Diamond! Diamond! Come and taste this." Gina waited for a minute and then she walked back to Diamond's bedroom. Gina stuck her head inside the room.

"Diamond, what did I tell you about snooping on people with that damn thing."

Diamond was looking out the telescope, "Mom, I'm not snooping. I'm working on my school project. Damn, she gets on my last nerve," she said under her breath as she slammed her bedroom door in her mom's face.

"What did you say?" Gina opened the bedroom door.

"Nothing, I'm trying to work on my school project."

"Slam this door in my face one more time and keep running that smart mouth of yours, and I will knock your ass into next year.

Diamond rolled her eyes again and turned her head. Gina walked out of the room, slamming the door behind her as her son Johnny walked into the apartment with an envelope in hand.

"I don't know what's wrong with your sister. She acts like she done lost her damn mind."

"Mom, Mr. Johnson said for you to call him, and he told me to give this to you." Johnny gave the envelope to his mom.

"What is it?"

"I don't know; open it."

Johnny sat down on the couch and turned the TV on and flicked through the channels. Gina sat down in the chair and opened the envelope. She put her hand up to her mouth as she looked at the one hundred-dollar bills.

"Oh, my God! This man is crazy! I told him I was not interested in him. Maybe if he had a legal job, I would go out with him."

Gina counted the money, "One hundred, two hundred, three hundred, four hundred, and five hundred. Jeez, there are fifteen hundred-dollar bills here. Damn, I sure could use this right about now."

Gina sat there for a minute staring at the money before placing the bills neatly back into the envelope and inside pocket.

Four young men walk toward the side of the gas station. JJ handed Harry the 38, Harry hesitated to take the gun.

"Man, you have to do this if you want to be a part of the family," JJ said holding the gun.

"Why do I have to do this? Isn't there something else I can do," Harry asked.

"Nope, I had to do it. Everyone had to do it. See my teardrops?"

Lil Moe moved closer to Harry so he could see the teardrops right below his left eye. "That means I did it three times. Man, just do it, and be done with it."

"Look, here he comes," JJ said.

The men turned to face the young man walking toward them

Diamond finished her dinner and headed back to her bedroom while Tonya went next door to play with her friends. Gina continued to sit at the table. She took the envelope out of her pocket, held it in her hand, and was debating whether to keep the money or return it.

Diamond flopped down onto her bed and was getting ready to finish her homework when she heard a noise outside.

Harry puts the gun in his pants.

"Harry, what are you doing? I know you're not backing out," JJ said.

"Come on, you big bitch," Lil Moe yelled. The men laughed loud enough for Diamond to hear. Diamond looked out her window and saw four guys standing on the side of the gas station messing around. She couldn't see who they were. She could only hear their laughter. She pulled her telescope closer to the window so she could see who the guys were and what they were doing. Diamond recognized the guys from hanging on the corner selling drugs, but she didn't know any of their names. Diamond turned her attention to the front of the gas station when she saw her friend Tyree walking toward the side of the building where the four guys were.

Ricky yanked Tyree's hat off of his head while Lil Moe snatched his bag and ran. Tyree ran after the guy who had his bag while the other three guys stood there laughing.

"Man, stop playing and give me my shit," Tyree yelled.

"And if I don't what are you going to do?" Lil Moe asked.

"If you don't give me my shit, you will find out," Tyree said with much anger in his voice. Tyree ran up to the guy and punched him in the face.

"Now I told you to stop playing, Lil nigga," Tyree said as he snatched his bag from him.

The other three guys didn't like the fact that Tyree had punched their friend. So the big guy pulled a gun from his pants and pointed it at Tyree. Diamond jumped when she saw the gun. She ran over to the wall and flicked the light switch off. She ran back to the telescope and continued to watch. The men continued to argue.

"Do it, Harry, kill this nigga," JJ egged him on.

"Why don't you do it?" Tyree said.

"Tyree, get out of there," Diamond yelled!

"Really, this nigga here doesn't know who he's talking to," JJ laughed. JJ snatched the gun from Harry and walked up to Tyree.

JJ pointed the gun to his forehead and pulled the trigger.

"Nigga, you should have asked somebody about me," JJ said. Diamond stood there and watched as her best friend fell to the ground.

13

"Oh my God!" Diamond screamed loud. Gina opened Diamond's bedroom door and flicked the light switch on.

The young men looked up at the window when they heard Diamond's scream and saw someone looking down at them.

"Mom! Turn the light off!" Diamond screamed.

"Why, what's going on?"

Diamond ran over and flicked the light switch off. She ran back over to the window in disbelief. She watched as the four guys looked up at the window, and then they started running toward the apartment building.

"Oh my God, mom! We have got to get out of here!"

"Diamond, what is going on?"

"They shot Tyree," Diamond cried.

"What are you talking about and who shot Tyree?"

Just then, Diamond's brother walked into the room.

"Hey, what's going on?" Johnny asked.

Diamond was busy looking for her purse. "I don't have time to explain. We need to leave now! Where's Tonya?"

"She's next door," her brother responded.

"Johnny, can you get her and bring her over to Mr. Johnson's. Hurry, I will explain everything once you get there. Mom, get your purse. We have to make sure we turn off all the lights."

"Diamond, what's going on? You are scaring me," Gina said frantically.

"If we don't get out of here, they will kill us!"

Once everyone made it to Mr. Johnson, Diamond explained what had happened. "They ran over here and are probably in the building somewhere."

CHAPTER TWO

JJ and his boys ran into the apartment building. They stood in the stairwell talking. They couldn't be sure which apartment they saw the person who was looking out at them in, but they had every intention of checking each apartment.

"Since we know, the apartment is on the fourth floor, and the window faces the gas station; it shouldn't be too hard to locate," JJ said.

"Are you sure it's on the fourth floor and not the fifth?" Harry asked.

JJ thought for a second, "No, I can't be sure, so let's start on the fourth floor and work our way up."

"So are we kicking in doors?" Lil Moe asked.

"Hell yeah, If that's the only way in!" Harry yelled!

Back in Ronnie's apartment

"You guys stay here, let me check things out."

Ronnie walked passed the stairwell, and as he did, he heard someone talking so he cracked open the door, eased inside the stairwell and stood. He peered over the rails to see the four men standing. He moved back and listened to their conversation.

"Okay, Lil Moe, I want you to stand guard around back and make sure no one leaves," JJ said.

"Ricky, I want you to stand guard here in front and make sure no one enters or leaves. Harry and I will check each apartment and if anyone tries to leave," JJ looked at the two with a serious face, "Kill em!"

Ronnie eased back inside the apartment hallway and gently shut the stairwell door. He made it inside his apartment and went straight to his closet in the hallway and opened the door. He pulled out two semi-automatics.

"Johnny, come here for a minute," Ronnie yelled.

Johnny got up off the couch and walked down the hall to where Ronnie stood holding two guns.

He handed Johnny a gun, "Do you know how to use this?"

16

"No, why?"

"Well, let me give you a quick lesson." He showed him quickly how to load the magazine, then rack the slide.

"Now all you need to do is point and shoot. You got it?"

"Let me try it," Johnny said. Johnny pulled out the magazine, reinserted the magazine clip, racked the slide and was ready to go.

"Now, it's you and your family's life or the men outside, and I know how much you love your family. I know you're a good kid and I hate to do this to you, but it's life or death for all of us."

"I'll do whatever it takes to protect my family." Johnny put the gun inside his pants and covered it with his shirt. Johnnie and Ronnie walked back into the living room with the others.

"Mr. Johnson, can we please call the paramedics for Tyree, he may still be alive?" Diamond pleaded.

"Diamond, I know he's your best friend, but if we call the paramedic's they will know exactly where you are calling from, and then the police will show up here letting the guys outside know who and where we are. I am so sorry, but we can't do that."

"Mom, this is not right. We can't just let him lay there. Would you want someone to do one of us like that?" Diamond cried.

"She's right, Ronnie. We have to take that chance. As a mother and as a human being, I can't do that to someone's child, and besides, he was like a son to me. I can't just sit here and do nothing while he is lying over there, I can't and I will not do it," Gina said.

Gina paced back and forth as she made the call requesting the paramedics. And right afterward, they heard a noise outside in the hall. Ronnie moved to the front door and looked out the peephole. He turned around with his finger up to his mouth.

"Shhhh."

They heard a door being kicked in. They listen to people screaming. The men searched apartment after apartment. They didn't know who they were looking for until they kicked in Gina's door. Once they were inside, they moved to each room until they came to the room with the telescope in it.

"Bingo!" J.J said. "Now we have to find out who lives here. Look around this motherfucker and see if we can find some family pictures."

"Well, we know they didn't walk up out of here, so they have to be hiding in someone's apartment," Harry said.

"That's why we will check every apartment on this floor," JJ said. Ronnie turned around and looked at Gina, "They're in your apartment right now. Did you leave the telescope out?"

"Oh my God!" I was in such a hurry to get out of there. I forgot all about it."

"See, I told you snooping would get your little ass in trouble. Now we are all in trouble behind your nosiness!" Gina yelled.

"I was in such a hurry. I'm sorry!"

"We need to find a way out of here and now," Ronnie said.

"If we can make it to the floor below us, my friend Jess will help us out."

"But how can we leave without them seeing us?"
Ronnie walked over to his kitchen window, opened it and stuck his head out to get a better view.

He stuck his head back in, "The fire escape, we can use the fire escape."

"The fire escape?" Gina said.

"It's that, are we stay here and wait for them to kick in my door," Ronnie said. They heard another door being kicked in. The men are getting closer to Ronnie's door.

"Okay, let's go!" Gina hopped up off the couch.

"Let me go first to make sure Jess is home, and once I am in, you guys will have to hurry."
Ronnie went down the fire escape until he was at his friend's kitchen window. He knocked on the window once and then twice and was getting ready to knock a third time when his friend came to the window.

"Man, what the hell are you doing out there?" Jess asked.

"I don't have time to explain, but I need your help."

"Whatever you need, you know I got you."
Ronnie stuck his head out the window and waved to Gina for her to come down.

"Diamond, I want you to take your sister with you and then Johnny, I want you to go."

"No mom, you take Tonya with you. This is all my fault, so I will be the last one to go."

"No, I will. I'm the man of the house, and I am here to protect my family." Diamond gave her brother a big hug, "I love you."

"Me too."

They both laughed.

"Mom, go ahead."

Gina eased out of the window and reached inside for Tonya and walked down the fire escape to the floor below. Ronnie helped them in.

"Diamond, now you go."

Diamond was safely inside when Johnny made his way out the window. He heard the someone trying to kick in the door. He rushed down the fire escape and inside Jess apartment.

"They're in your apartment right now."

"Did you shut the kitchen window?"

"Yep, sure did."

"Thank God. Now they have no way of knowing we are down here. I hope they don't find my stash because if they do then it will be some real shit going down."

Once they were all safely inside Jess apartment, Ronnie explained everything to him.

"So, how many guys are there?"

"Four."

Jess paced back and forth, "Do you know these guys?"

"No, but I've seen them around selling drugs on the corner from time to time."

"Okay, we should be good then. All we have to do is sit tight and wait until they leave," Jess said.

"Well, it's not that simple since the telescope was left out. I am pretty sure they saw it when they checked the apartment, so they know she didn't leave. And they have two men guarding the front and the back entrance."

"Yeah, you're probably right. Well, we can do two things, I can call my boys over which may cause a problem or I can go out and pull the fire alarm, and we can sit here and wait for the fire department and the police to show up to make our exit."

"I say we do both. You call your boys, and I'll call mine," Ronnie said.

Once the plan was in place. Jess walked out into the hallway. He walked about four feet until he was standing directly in front of the fire alarm. He looked around and saw the coast was clear. He pulled the lever, and once the alarm sounded, he rushed back inside his apartment and waited.

Jess walked back into his bedroom and looked out the window to see what was going on outside. He looked across the street to the gas station and saw police cars and people standing outside watching. He watched as the ambulance loaded the body into the ambulance. He saw the body bag which told him Tyree was dead.

"Damn!" He said as he shook his head.

Denise Hill
The Window

21

CHAPTER THREE

Inside Jess' apartment

They remained inside the apartment for about twenty to twenty-five minutes until the fire department evacuated the building. Gina walked in front with her youngest daughter Tonya, while Jess and Ronnie walked on each side of Diamond and Johnny took up the rear. They thought they were in the clear until they stepped foot outside the building in the back where the cars were parked. Diamond jumped when she saw the big guy standing there looking directly at her smiling with the other three guys and a police officer while shaking his head and holding a picture of her and her family.

"Keep walking, Diamond and don't look at anyone."

"Too late, he knows who I am."

"What?" Jess asked.

"Didn't you see the picture of my family and me in his hand?"

"Don't worry about it, you're safe, just keep walking," Jess tried to assure her. They were thankful for the police officers that were out back and just then, their boy's pulled up.

"Follow us," Ronnie said as he motioned to the men. Ronnie walked to the driver's side of his car.

"Diamond, I want you to get in the back," Ronnie told her.

Jess and his boys followed behind Ronnie and his boys.

The police officer that was talking to Ricky and his boys took down Ronnie's license plate number and continued to stand and talk with them.

"You guys need to be cool and let me handle things. I'll let you know when it's time to make our move," Officer Smith said.

"Right on, cuz," JJ said.

An hour later, they turned the corner onto a street full of big beautiful houses.

"Where are we going?" Diamond asked.

"Somewhere where we will all be safe until we come up with a plan," Ronnie said as he continued to drive until they came to a house that looked like a mansion. It was humongous. Ronnie pulled up, punched in his password, and hit the enter button. The Iron Gate opened, and once the last car was through, the gate closed.

Inside the home, Gina and her family looked around the house in disbelief. Make yourself at home. This place will be your home until we can take care of things.

"Mom, this place is fantastic," Johnny said as he continued to look around.

Gina looked over at Ronnie. She walked over to him, "Whose house does this belong to?"

"It's ours for the time being." Ronnie didn't want to tell Gina just yet that this was his home. He had a feeling that once she found out, she wouldn't stay.

"Come, let me show you guys where you'll be sleeping."

Ronnie escorted them upstairs. "Gina, this will be your room and right next to it, will be Diamond's and Tonya's room. Johnny, your room is next to mine on the other side of the stairs. Get comfortable, and I will see you guys in the morning."

Downstairs in the family room, the men gathered to talk.

"I'm going back to the apartment to get some of your moms and your sister's clothing. Do you want to come with us?"

"Yeah, there are some things I need to get."

"Jerome, Trent, and Ralph, I want you guys to stay here with the women."

Ronnie, Jess, Johnny, and two other guys sat outside the apartment building checking out the surroundings before heading inside.

Later that night, Diamond awakened as she heard her sister call out to her.

"Diamond, Diamond, are you awake? I have to go to the bathroom."

Diamond got up and walked Tonya to the restroom. After putting Tonya back to bed, Diamond wanted to see if anyone else was up in the house. Diamond stood in the hallway looking around before heading down the stairs. As she made her way downstairs, she heard voices coming from a room. She walked down the hall, following the sound of voices when she came to a room with three guys. One was sitting down watching TV, and the other two were standing at the table while sending money through a money counter. As she moved to stand in the doorway, the tall, handsome one looked up, "What are you doing down here?" The handsome one asked.

"I couldn't sleep so I came down here to see if anyone else was up."

"Do you need something? Are you hungry?"

"No, I'm good." Diamond said smiling.

The two stood there eyeing each other when the two other men started laughing. Jerome looked at the men and walked toward Diamond.

"Hey, let me walk you back to your room."

"Your name is Diamond, right?"

"Yes, and you are?"

"I'm Jerome, but you can call me Rome."

"Okay, Rome, but whose money was that down there?" Jerome laughed.

"I see you're nosey."

"Pretty much, and that's what got me in this mess now, being nosey. So, are you a drug dealer?"

"I see you have a lot of questions. Diamond, there are some things you need know."

"If I'm going to be around drug dealers, don't you think I need to know this?"

"You will know what you need to know in due time. So why don't you take your pretty little self in your room and get some rest."

"Oh, so you think I'm pretty?" Diamond asked as she flirted with the young man.

Jerome laughed as he moved closer to Diamond and planted a kiss on her forehead.

"Yes, and good night, Diamond."

Jerome stood there until she was inside before walking down the hallway and heading back downstairs.

Ronnie and the men got out and walked into the apartment building. They walked down the hallway, and was walking toward the elevator, when they ran into JJ and his boys, but this time there were four more of them.

"Hey, aren't you that OG that lives on the fourth floor?" JJ asked. Ronnie nodded his head. JJ's boys stood in front of the elevator.

"Hey, let them through, except for that little nigga, he's staying with us," JJ said.

Ronnie and his men stopped in their tracks and formed a circle around Johnny. They thought about pulling their guns out, but since JJ and his boys already had their weapons drawn, it wouldn't have done them any good.

"You guys don't want to do this. We didn't come here for any trouble. We came to get a few things, and that's it," Ronnie said.

"If you and your men want out of here alive, you will do as I say and leave that little nigga with us," JJ yelled.

"Naw, that's not happening," Jess said.

"Okay, have it your way."

Ronnie looked around the hallway, trying to think of a plan when he saw the stairwell. Ronnie whispered, "On the count of three head for the stairwell. One, two, three." On the count of three, Ronnie grabbed Johnny as the men rushed into the stairwell. JJ's and his boys started shooting while some of them hopped on the elevator.

The men ran for their lives as they headed for the fourth floor.

Denise Hill
The Window

CHAPTER FOUR

Inside the elevator, the men stood in silence until they reached the fourth floor. They exited the elevator and stood in front of the stairwell waiting for Ronnie and his men to exit.

Inside the stairwell Jess thought of something, "Hey, what if they are waiting on us to exit the stairwell on your floor?"

"I didn't think about that."

"Let's go to my apartment since they are not expecting us to go there," Jess suggested.

Inside Jess's apartment, he paced back and forth trying to come up with a plan, "We will have to call for reinforcement if we want to make it out of here alive."

"Let's do it, but first I want to go to my apartment and to Gina's," Ronnie said.

Ronnie took the fire escape up to his kitchen window. He slowly raised the window and climbed inside. Ronnie stood there quietly listening for any sounds of movements inside his apartment, and when heard nothing, he moved to the living room and saw his front door opened. He peered out the door to see if he saw anyone. He saw four men standing by the stairwell three doors down from his apartment. Ronnie eased out of the door. He slowly moved to Gina's apartment as he continued to look back at the guys, and when Ronnie came to Gina's door, which had been kicked open, he entered. Ronnie walked inside and saw her apartment in shambles. He went to Gina's room and grabbed a suitcase out of the closet and began packing some of her things. Then Ronnie went to Diamond and Tonya's room and gathered some of their belongings. As he made his way to Johnny's room, he heard voices outside the door.

"Where the hell are they?" Ricky asked.

"Maybe they exited on the floor below us or above us," Harry suggested.

"Yeah, they could be waiting for us to leave. Why don't we make them think we've given up and go across the street and wait for them to come out?" Ricky said.

Ronnie stood as he heard the men board the elevator before going to Johnny's room. Ronnie grabbed some of Johnny's things and put them into the suitcase.

27

Ronnie made his way back to his apartment where he grabbed his dope. He opened the black duffel bag to make sure his money was there before heading down to Jess's place.

When Ronnie walked in, he found the men standing there watching the news. Johnny looked up.

"They're talking about Tyree. The person they interviewed lied and said it was a drive-by shooting."

"That's a shame. Hey, I got some things for you, your mom and your sisters, but we have a problem. The men want us to think they have left the building. They're across the street somewhere, waiting for us to walk outside."

"That's not a problem. All we need to do is to make it to the next block and have some of our men meet us there. We will come back for your car tomorrow afternoon," Jess said.

"Great idea, make that call, but find out how long it will take them to get here so we won't be standing out there like sitting ducks, and tell them to bring the Yukon."

The men made their way out of the building through the back way and headed for the next street over to the bowling alley parking lot. The men arrived at the bowling alley and stood on the side of the building until they saw two cars pull up. Once they recognized the men, they emerged from the side of the building and hopped inside the vehicle. Ronnie and Jess and Johnnie hopped in the first car, while the other two guys jumped in the second car.

Ronnie and Jess told their buddies what had happened.

"Are you shitting me?" Leon asked.

"Damn, this is some movie shit," Donnie chimed in.

"Them niggas don't know who they are fucking with," Jess said.

"Hey, pull over here for a minute. I want to see where these niggas are hiding out," Ronnie said.

The cars pulled over, and they sat there for a couple of minutes, then they saw someone run across the street from the apartment building. They also saw a police car.

"There they are. Hey, isn't that the cop we saw talking to them earlier?" Jess asked.

"Yep, that's him. Ride past them, but ride slow. I want to see something," Ronnie said. Ronnie thought he saw a gang member with them. As the car drove past the men, Ronnie recognized the gang member.

"Just as I suspected. I knew that Lil dude looked familiar. They are part of the Warlord gang. And you know it's about a million of them," Ronnie said.

"Remember when we had that run in with them about ten years ago?" Leon asked Donnie.

"Yes, and it wasn't good. If it wasn't for my friend who has passed away, there's no telling how it would have ended."

"So what did he do to help you guys out?" Ronnie asked.

"His cousin was the leader of the Warlord gang, and because the other rival gang members knew he was related to him, they hated him too. One day he was coming out of the grocery store, and six gang members were waiting for him. I sat in my car and watched them prepare to kill him. I pulled up on the sidewalk and yelled for him to get in my car and we took off. He never forgot that. He said he would owe me for the rest of his life. So when he found out that there was bad blood between the Warlords and us, he went to his cousin, and our beef ended, but now that he's gone, I don't know if I still have that pull," Donnie told Ronnie.

"Well, you know it won't hurt to see what he can do, because I will give my life for Gina and her kids," Ronnie said.

"Let's hope it doesn't come to that," Jess said.

"Pull up right next to my car. I'm will drive my car back, and hopefully, they won't try to follow me back, but make sure you hit the light so they can't see inside."

Leon looked back at Ronnie, "If they do, we will distract them until you get away and we will meet you at your place a little later." Ronnie got out of the car and slid in behind the wheel of his car and started the ignition and took off.

Three guys emerged from the darkness and stood by Lil Moe and the police officer and watched as Ronnie pulled off.

"You need to follow that nigga," JJ said.

"For what, I already know where he lives," Officer Smith told him.

"Well, let's go!" Harry yelled.

"Hold your horses," Officer Smith said.

Officer Smith puts his hand up to hold Harry back.

"And why are you all in this, from what I heard you were to damn scared to pull the trigger?" Officer Smith told Harry.

Harry stepped back with his head down.

"Anyway, I told you guys I would take care of this. Just hold tight. I want them to think everything is cool, and when they least expect it, that's when we will kill all of them, and besides, you motherfuckers will mess everything up, and I cannot afford to lose my job over this shit," Officer Smith told them.

Denise Hill
The Window

CHAPTER FIVE

The next morning, Diamond was the last one to awake. Everyone was downstairs having breakfast when she walked in. Gina looked up, "Good morning."

"Good morning," Diamond said. Thanks Mr. Johnson for bringing my things from the apartment."
Ronnie nodded and smiled.

"Are you hungry?" Gina asked Diamond.

"No."

"Diamond, eat something sweetheart. I know you're hurting, but you still need to take care of yourself." Gina walked over and hugged her daughter.

"Has anyone watched the news to see if Tyree is alive?"
Jess hesitated, "I hate to be the one to tell you this, but when we were at my apartment last night, I saw them put a body in a body bag and later we saw on the news that someone at the gas station had been murdered. They said it was a drive-by shooting."
Diamond cried, "That's a bunch of bull! I knew I should have done something. I should have called the paramedics right when it happened. And maybe he would still be alive." Diamond ran upstairs to her room in tears.

"So, what's the plan? I know we will not sit inside this house forever?" Jess asked.

"I know the kids have to go to school," Gina said.

"I'm okay if I don't go back," Johnny said.
Laughter filled the room.

"You know your sister will die if she can't go back to school and besides, you only have eight months left."

"So what grade are you guys in?" Jess asked.

"Diamond and I are seniors and Tonya is in the third grade."
Jess looked strange, "Are you guy's twins or something?"
The room filled with laughter again.

"Now you know damn well they are not twins," Gina said.
Jerome walked over to Ronnie, "What's the deal, Ron, you have been sitting over here all quiet?" Jerome asked.

"Just thinking young man, just thinking," Ronnie looked up at Jerome.

"What are you thinking about?"

"Thinking about how to get us out of this alive and well. Donnie, how difficult will it be for you to contact the leader of the Warlords?" Ronnie asked.

"It shouldn't be too hard. I know he owns a car lot on the Westside."

"I need a meeting with him ASAP!"

"Let me see what I can do. He should be there around 9 or 10 this morning."

Upstairs in the bedroom, Diamond heard a knock at the door. She got up off the bed and walked over and opened the door. It surprised to see Jerome.

"Are you okay?"

"No, not really."

"Can I come in?"

"Sure." Diamond walked over and sat on the side of the bed. Jerome followed behind her and sat next to her.

"Diamond, is there anything I can do to make you feel better?"

Diamond looked up.

"Do you have a car?"

"Yes, why?"

"I want to see my friends, family, but I don't want anyone to know that I am going."

"Do you think that's a good idea?"

"It's something that I have to do. I have to do right by him."

"What do you mean; do right by him?"

"I want the person responsible for his death behind bars."

"I think you need to chill out for a minute. You might make things worse."

"Well, if you don't want to take me, I will find another way over there."

Jerome thought about what he was about to do.

"I can take you, but you could put all of our lives in danger."

"How? No one will see me."

"Let's hope not. And how are we just going to walk up out of here with no one seeing us?"

33

"Come on Rome, I'm sure you can think of a way for us to get away from here for a little while," Diamond moved closer to him and ran a finger down the side of his face.

Jerome laughed, "You think you slick, don't you?"

"Why I gotta be slick?"

Jerome pulled Diamond's face close to his and brushed his lips up against her lips to see how she would react. When he pulled away, Diamond looked at him, "Did you think it would scare me? Did you think I would back away from you?" Diamond asked as she admired the handsome young man.

"How old are you?"

"I'm almost eighteen."

"When's your birthday?"

"In a few months."

"In a few months?" Jerome repeated.

"Yes, my birthday is December 16. Why are you going to buy me a birthday gift?"

"Maybe, maybe not."

"So, are you going to take me or not?"

"I'll take you. When do you want to go?"

"In a couple of hours."

"All right, in the meantime, think about how you will sneak out of here."

Diamond walked Jerome to the door. Jerome reached over and kissed Diamond on the lips and walked out, shutting the door behind him. As Jerome walked out, Gina caught him and stopped him on his way out.

"What the hell are you doing in there with my daughter?"

"I was checking on her, making sure she was all right."

"Is she okay?"

"Yeah, she's good?"

Jerome walked away and headed back downstairs to think of a way to get Diamond out of the house.

Gina knocked at Diamond's door. Diamond walked over to the door.

"What, don't tell me you want another kiss?" Diamond said as she opened the door and stood there embarrassed.

"What were you and that boy doing in here?"

"Mom, please, not now," Diamond said with an attitude.

"What do you mean not now? Girl, don't you know I will hurt your little ass. We are in so much trouble because of you, and you got the nerve to have an attitude with me?"

"Mom, I'm sorry, I'm upset and hurt. I kind of feel responsible for Tyree's death."

"Diamond, you are not responsible for his death. You weren't even with him."

"I know, but he was at the gas station because of me."
Diamond thought back to her phone conversation with Tyree.

"Why don't you stop at the gas station before coming over and buy us some hot Cheetos and pop. Oh, and don't forget the gummy bears."

"What is up with you and those damn gummy bears?"
Diamond cried, "If it weren't for me, he would still be alive, and we wouldn't be in this mess."
Gina wiped the tears from Diamond's face.

"Honey, you had no way of knowing those guys would be there. Everyone knows how much you cared for Tyree. We know you would have never put him in a dangerous situation on purpose."

"Mom, I feel like I have lost a part of me. Tyree and I had been friends since I was three years old. I wish we wouldn't have moved then I would still have my friend."
Gina hugged her daughter tightly, "I wish I could take your pain away. You know Tyree was like a son to me, and I will miss him dearly. My heart goes out to his family, especially Sheila. I know she's having a time with this. I wish I could be there for her."

Denise Hill
The Window

36

CHAPTER SIX

Ronnie, Jess, Leon, Donnie, and a couple of other guys pulled up to the car dealership owned by the leader of the warlord gang. The men were all strapped just in case things went south. Three men got out of each car and walked toward the front door. Inside the dealership, Deon and his men stood inside and watched as the men made their way inside the building. Donnie and Leon led the way.

Jerome pulled out the gate and drove off. Diamond raised from the back seat.

"See, I told you this would work."

Jerome laughed.

"You're a sneaky little something, I see. So where are we going?"

"We are going to 3845 N. LaSalle Street on the east side. Hey, pull over so I can get in the front."

"I see you're bossy too."

"Whatever."

Jerome pulled over and Diamond got out of the back and into the passenger seat. They had no idea that someone was tailing them.

An hour later, Jerome turned onto LaSalle and slowly made his way down the street.

"I should park two or three houses down from their house just in case people are watching. Put your phone number in my phone in case some shit goes down while you're inside."

Jerome handed Diamond his phone. Jerome checked Diamond out as she locked her number in his phone. He noticed that she looked like a darker version of Ashanti.

Diamond looked over at him and handed him his phone back.

Diamond smiled, "Take a picture; it will last longer."

Jerome chuckled, "I might do that. So what's the plan? Do I need to go in there with you?"

"No, stay out here and if you see a gang of guys, call me, and I will leave out the back way, and you can meet me at the entrance of the alley on the side street back there." Diamond pointed.

"How long will you be?"

"Not too long."

"I hope you know what you're doing."

"I got this. I'll be right back."
Diamond got out of the car and pulled her hood over her head and strolled casually down the street until she came to Tyree's house. Diamond looked around at her surroundings before walking up the walkway.
Diamond knocked a couple of times before a tear-filled eye Sheila opened the door.

"Hey Ms. Sheila, how are you? I am so sorry for your loss, and I wish I would have known what would happen."

"Hey baby, come on in." Diamond and Ms. Sheila walked into the den. Ms. Sheila sat in her lazy boy, "Diamond, what did you mean you wish you would have known?"
Just then, Tyree's sister and brother walked into the room.
Tyree's sister yelled, "Are you responsible for my brother's death?"

"Tyree and I were on the phone right before. He was coming over, and I asked him to stop at the gas station to get us some snacks. I wish I wouldn't have asked him to stop; he would still be here."

"I know you and Tyree loved you some Cheetos," Ms. Sheila said as a tear rolled down her face.

"Do you know who killed him?" Tyree's sister continued to question Diamond, "you didn't answer my question Diamond!"
Diamond and Tyree's sister have never gotten along.

"Why don't you ask your boyfriend? I have seen him with those guys a couple of times."

"So you know who killed him?" Nick, Tyree's brother, asked Diamond.

"I saw it go down, but I don't know the guy's name, I've seen him a couple of times hanging on the corner selling drugs. But her dude knows who he is."
Diamond looked at Tracy. Just then, her dude walked through the door. He eyed Diamond strangely, to the point she felt uncomfortable.

"What'd up Diamond?" Jason asked.

"Hey, Jason."

"I have to go, but call me once you've made the funeral arrangements."
Diamond hugged Sheila and walked outside. Jason walked outside with Diamond and grabbed hold of her arm. Jerome saw this happening and hopped out of the car and ran to Diamonds rescue.

"If you know what's good for you and your family, you will keep your fucking mouth shut."

"And if you know what's good for you, you will get your ass out of my damn way." Diamond said as she jerked away from Jason and tried to move, but he blocked her path.

"Hey, is there a problem here?" Jerome ran up onto the porch. Jason turned to look at Jerome. The men stood there eyeing each other.

"Is there a problem Diamond?"

"Come on, let's go!" Diamond said as she reached for Jerome's arm. Diamond and Jerome made their way off the porch and down the street. Just then, Jerome noticed a police car parked across the street and the same police officer from the apartments sitting inside watching them.

"Shit!"

"What's wrong?"

"Nothing, hurry and get in."

"Jerome, what's going on?"

"I knew coming here was a bad idea. Don't look now, but the same police officer from the apartments last night is sitting in that police car across the street."

"Damn!"

"What the hell happened back there and who was that guy and why was he grabbing on you?"
Jerome pulled off, checking his surroundings and making sure the cop didn't follow them.

"He's friends with the guy that killed Tyree, and he's dating Tyree's sister. He told me to keep my damn mouth shut. I can't believe him, and when I told Tyree's sister that her dude knew who killed Tyree, she said nothing she didn't even question him when he walked in. Tyree's mother didn't say anything. How could they do Tyree like that! That motherfucker will pay for what he did. I promise you that," Diamond said angrily.

"Calm down, everything will be handled, but you cannot let anyone know I brought you here today, okay?"

"I won't; I promise and thank you."
Jerome looked over at Diamond. He couldn't believe how much she looked like Ashanti.

"You owe me."

"And what do I owe you?"
Jerome laughed.
"I'll show you later tonight."

Denise Hill
The Window

41

CHAPTER SEVEN

"**What's** up, Donnie? What's up, Leon," Deon said.

Ronnie and his men lay back as Leon and Donnie made their way closer to the leader.

"Hey Deon, I'm glad you could meet with us on such short notice," Donnie said.

"No problem. Follow me into my office."

"Let me introduce you to some people first. They're the reason we are here," Leon said.

Leon and Donnie turned to face Ronnie, Jess, and the others.

Donnie did the introductions, "Deon, this is Ronnie, Jess, Trent, and Malcolm."

"Follow me." Deon nodded.

The men followed Deon into his office. He motioned for them to sit. Deon took a seat behind his desk.

"Would anyone care for a drink?" Deon asked.

"Naw, we good. I want to talk to you about a murder one of your young men committed. Someone that I cared dearly for, daughter saw everything, it was her best friend that one of your men murdered. I want to make sure this family stays safe," Ronnie said. "As you already know they kicked in their apartment door looking for them and early this morning, we had a run in with them. We don't want any trouble."

Deon never looked up as he picked up a cigar box, opened it and took a cigar out. He cut the end off and lit it.

"Would anyone care for one?" Deon asked as he looked up.

"I need to make sure this family stays safe," Ronnie repeated himself.

"Well, that all depends on her. I can't have any of my men going to prison," Deon replied.

"Man, this was her best friend we're talking about. He was an innocent young man killed for no reason!" Ronnie said.

"And like I said, it depends on if she keeps her mouth shut, her family will be safe."

"So, it's okay with you when your men murder innocent people?" Deon threw his hands up.

"Let's get out of here," Ronnie said. The men got up to walk out.

"Remember what I said," Deon said as he eyed Ronnie.

Ronnie looked back at him and shook his head before walking out the door.

Once inside the car, Ronnie looked at Jess, "That motherfucker has no regard for anyone's life."

"I don't trust him as far as I can see him."

The men drove off, heading back to the house.

Jerome pulled onto the street that Ronnie lived on and pulled over.

"I need for you to get in the back and stay down until I get out of the car. I will leave the back door unlocked so you can get in."

The police officer parked as he sat and watched as Diamond got out of the front seat and into the back seat.

"What are those two doing?" Officer Smith asked himself.

The police car followed behind, careful not to be noticed.

Jerome pulled around back, got out of the car and entered the house to find Gina in between the hallway and family room.

Gina walked up to him, "Have you seen Diamond?"

"She was out back the last time I saw her."

Gina looked at Jerome strange. She knew something was up with him and her daughter. As she walked away, Diamond walked through the door.

Gina heard the door opened and turned to see Diamond, "Where have you been? I've been looking all over for you?"

Jerome turned to see Diamond and mouthed the word out back.

Diamond looked at Jerome before answering.

"I was out back."

Gina looked back at Jerome. Jerome turned and walked away.

"Um," Gina said.

Diamond walked past her mom smiling.

"What's up big head?" Diamond walked past her brother and pushed his head.

"You two ain't slick," Johnny whispered.

"Whatever." Diamond said as she rolled her neck,

Ronnie and the men pulled up to the gate. Ronnie punched in the code that unlocked the black Iron Gate. Once the gate opened, the men drove through and drove around back.

The police car sat parked on the side street and watched as the men pulled in and drove around back.

The back door opened and Gina waited for the men to walk in. By the look on Ronnie's face, she could tell something was up.

Gina got up and walked over to Ronnie, "How did it go?"

Ronnie grabbed a hold of Gina's hand and took her downstairs. He took her to his security room.

Gina walked in and looked around the room, "Oh my God! What are all these cameras for?"

"These cameras keep me informed on what's going on outside my home when I am here or away."

"Are you in some kind of trouble?"

Ronnie laughed, "No, but in the line of work that I am in, you can't be too careful."

"So, do you mean to tell me that this is your home?"

Ronnie eyed Gina closely as he shook his head.

Gina folded her arms across her chest.

"Ronnie, be honest with me. Are me and my kids safe here?"

"Of course you and your family are safe. I would not have brought you here if you weren't, but I need to talk to you about our meeting today. We met with the leader of the Warlord gang. One of their members killed Tyree. I went to ask the leader to guarantee protection for you and your family."

"Okay, so what did he say?"

Ronnie moved to sit behind the desk and rewound the cameras so he can see what happened while he was away.

"He said you guys would be safe as long as Diamond keeps her mouth shut about what happened, but I don't trust that dude, but we will see."

Ronnie stopped the camera when he saw Jerome leaving and fast forwarded until he saw him coming back. He watched as Jerome walk inside and then he saw Diamond get out of the back and stepped inside.

Ronnie looked up at Gina.

"Where did Jerome and Diamond go to?"

"What are you talking about? Jerome left by himself."

Ronnie looked at her without saying a word.

"Why don't you believe the guy about us being safe?"

"He doesn't seem to care about anyone but himself, but I will give him the benefit of the doubt."

"Well, the kids need to go to school, and I need to go to work."

"I can arrange for a driver to drop you guys off and pick you up. I would feel much better if you guys stayed here a little longer to see how things go."

Later that evening after dinner, Ronnie pulled Jerome to the side in the hallway.

"Follow me, I want you to see something."

Jerome followed Ronnie downstairs to the security room.

Ronnie sat behind the cameras in his chair and pulled the footage up of him and Diamond.

"Can you explain this to me?"

Jerome forgot about the cameras in the back.

Jerome shook his head, "Damn! You got me. Diamond wanted to go to see her friend's family, and I knew if I didn't take her, she would find another way, and I didn't want to take any chances of her running into some guys from the Warlord gang, but she did, and if I hadn't been there, it could have gotten ugly."

Ronnie raised from the chair and stepped around to where Jerome stood.

"What happened?"

"Tyree's sister is dating a guy in the gang. He followed Diamond outside and grabbed her and told her to keep her mouth shut. But then I stepped in, and he backed down."

"Well, I'm glad you were there, but next time, don't take her anywhere. We have to be very careful and keep our eyes and ears open. Something tells me we will have a run-in with the gang members. Now, can I trust you to take her and her brother to school in the morning and picking them up in the afternoon?"

Jerome laughed a little, "Yes, you can trust me to do that."

Denise Hill
The Window

CHAPTER EIGHT

When Jerome thought everyone was asleep, he sent Diamond a text message. Diamond heard a beep letting her know that she received a message. Diamond looked at her phone and read the message:

"Meet me downstairs and be quiet."

Diamond got out of bed, careful not to wake her sister. She slowly opened her bedroom door and eased out, shutting it softly behind her. She made her way downstairs where she saw Jerome standing there, leaning up against the wall waiting for her. When he saw her, he smiled. He grabbed Diamond by the hand and led her into the bedroom and shut the door. Ronnie sat behind the desk and watched Jerome and Diamond. He knew something was going on with those two. He only hoped Jerome was smart and that he protect her. Ronnie shut the camera down when they entered the bedroom. Ronnie shook his head. He was young once, so he understood. He wished that he and Gina could get together.

Music played in the background, 'Ice on My Baby' by Yung Bleu as Jerome pulled Diamond to him. He kissed her softly as he lifted her shirt up and over her head. He moved down to her perky breasts as he took one into his mouth. A moan escaped her mouth. Jerome took the other nipple into his mouth and sucked it until it became hard. Jerome picked her up, and she wrapped her legs around his waist as he moved toward the bed. Jerome laid her down and pulled her pajama pants off and pulled her closer to the edge of the bed. He looked down at her.

"Are you ready for me?"

Diamond was afraid she didn't know what to expect since this was her first time.

Diamond whispered, "I guess so."

"Don't worry, I will be gentle with you," Jerome promised.

Jerome removed his boxers as Diamond laid there admiring him. Seconds later, Jerome slid the tip inside her.

"No! Oh my God!" Diamond screamed as she tried to scoot up, but Jerome pulled her back.

"It's just the head. The pain won't last long."

Jerome moved slowly in and out, deeper and deeper.

Minutes later, Diamond screamed, "Oh my God! Jerome!"

"Does it feel good, baby?"

"Jerome, yes!" Diamond moaned.

Jerome leaned forward and kissed her as he continued stroking her. His strokes become faster and faster. He rolled over, pulling her with him until she was on top. Diamond rode him.

"Damn, baby, give it to me!"

Diamond rode the hell out of him, and all at once she screamed as the thunderous orgasm ran through her body. Jerome shook with convulsions as the feeling hit him. Minutes later, Diamond eased off of Jerome and laid next to him.

"So, how did it feel?"

Jerome looked down at Diamond and ran his finger down the side of her face. Diamond looked up at him, "At first, it was painful, but then it got better."

Jerome laughed.

"Just wait, it gets even better."

Diamond laughed, "I can't wait."

Jerome pulled Diamond closer to him and kissed her. They lay there cuddling until they fell asleep.

Six hours later, Diamond's alarm went off. Diamond opened her eyes, glanced around the room, and looked up at Jerome and smiled.

"How long have you been awake?"

"For about an hour. What time does school start?"

"8:30, damn, I hope my mom's not awake."

"You know that I am taking you and your brother to school, right?"

"Yep," Diamond said as she kissed Jerome on the lips, jumped up, and put her pajamas on and headed upstairs.

Diamond opened the bedroom door to find her mom.

"And where the hell have you been?"

"I was downstairs in the kitchen getting something to drink."

Gina eyed Diamond, "You better not be messing around with that boy."

Diamond rolled her eyes, "Mom, I am almost 18 years old. I should be able to date whoever I want to date."

Diamond walked into the bathroom and shut the door. Gina continued helping Tonya get dressed.

"Finish dressing while Imake sure your brother is up." Gina walked over to the door.

"Mom, when are we going back to our apartment?"

Gina turned around, "Soon sweetheart, soon."

Parked outside the school, Jerome talked to Diamond and Johnny.

"Now, remember what we talked about, and if something doesn't feel right, it probably isn't, so I want you to get with each other and find a safe place and call me."

"All right, later," Johnny said as he got out of the car.

Diamond watched as her brother caught up with his friends.

"So, you're just going to sit here?"

Jerome smiled, looking over at her.

"I wish I could, but I can't. I just wanted a kiss, but not in front of my brother."

"Is that all you want?"

"No, but that will have to do me for right now."

Jerome leaned over and kissed Diamond. "That should hold you over until I see you again."

Diamond laughed, "Oh my God! Why did you have to kiss me like that?"

Diamond made her way out of the car, smiling from ear to ear.

"Have a great day!" Jerome said.

"Thanks, you too!"

Johnny and his friends walked inside the school.

"We heard what happened the other night. That's too bad about Tyree. Is it true did they kick in your apartment door looking for you guys?" Mike asked.

"I'm afraid so. Diamond saw it all go down."

"Some mean looking dudes were here looking for you and your sister," Fred told Johnny.

"When?"

"Yesterday, they were here at school and later around the apartment building," Fred said.

"Have you ever seen them before?"

"No, we haven't," Mike said, but I think they belong to the Warlord gang. That's what I heard.

49

"I'm surprised you're here today. You guys should lie low until things die down," Fred told Johnny.

"Everything should be cool now." The boys walked into their first class.

Denise Hill
The Window

CHAPTER NINE

Diamond walked into her classroom, and everyone stopped talking and looked at her.

"Look at the snitch."

Diamond turned around to look at Jennifer, "What did you say?"

"Never mind her. She's just mad because her boyfriend is a part of the gang that killed Tyree. I don't blame you, I would tell on their asses too." Paula said.

"But I have said anything to anyone."

"Well, the word on the street is that you told Tracy and her family who killed Tyree. Tracy's been running her mouth to the Warlords. You need to be careful."

"That stupid bitch. Thanks, Paula, for letting me know."

"Anytime, girl."

Later that afternoon, the mean looking dude and two guys entered the school. They began asking the students about Johnny and his sister, Diamond, again. Fred and Mike spotted the guys. Fred and Mike took off running in the hallway, looking for Johnny and his sister Diamond. They search the first floor and then the second floor when Fred saw Johnny talking to a female at her locker.

Fred out of breath said, "There he is."

Mike pulled Johnny to the side, "Hey, that dude is back, and he is with a couple of other dudes. He's asking about you and your sister again."

"Shit, where's Diamond. Let me call her," Johnny said nervously.

Diamond was talking with her math teacher, trying to get the assignments she missed when she received a call. She remembered what Jerome told her, so she excused herself.

"I'm sorry, but I have to take this."

Diamond walked over to the corner of the room.

"What's going on?"

"We have to go. There are some guys here from the Warlord gang asking about us."

"Where are you?" Diamond asked as she looked around at her surroundings.

"I'm heading to the gym, meet me there."

"Okay, I'm on my way."

"Is everything okay?" The teacher asked as she saw Diamond's facial expression. Some teachers had been talking in the teachers' lounge yesterday when they got word that some gang members were in the school yesterday looking for her and her brother.

"I'm sorry, but I have to go."

"Diamond, Diamond," the teacher called out to her. The teacher made her way to the entryway of the door and saw Diamond sprinting down the hall. The teacher was concerned for her and her brother's safety and notified the principal.

Diamond ran out and took the back way to get to the gym as quickly as she could.

Diamond opened the doors to the gym and walked inside to see the empty gym. Her heart dropped to her stomach as she looked around the gym.

"Oh my God! Johnny, where are you?" She said as she scanned the gym.

"Diamond up here."

Diamond looked up to see Johnny on the balcony. Diamond rushed to her brother.

"Johnny, now what is going on?"

"Diamond, we have to get out of here. Members of the Warlord gang are looking for us."

Just then, they heard some commotion outside the gym as Fred and Mike were pushed through the gym doors.

"Now, where the hell are they?" JJ asked.

"I don't know who you are talking about?" Fred lied.

"You know damn well who we are talking about," Ricky told him.

"Where are Johnny and Diamond?" JJ asked.

"We have no idea where they are," Mike replied.

Ricky punched Fred in the stomach and then looked over at Mike Diamond and Johnny stood back as they watched what was going on.

"We have got to get out of here," Johnny said nervously. Diamond sent a 911 text message to Jerome.

"Please, we don't know where they are. The last time I saw Johnny was when we were in our first class this morning." Mike said.

"You two better not be lying to us," JJ said.

Fred still holding his stomach, "We're not, I promise."

"Let's wait out front.," Ricky said.

The men walked outside the gym doors and stood looking around. They watched Fred and Mike walk away. They wanted to see where Fred and Mike would run off to. Fred and Mike walked outside the gym and down the hall to their last class.

Jerome and his worker were on the corner collecting money from one of his soldiers when he received a 911 message from Diamond.

"Damn! I got to go. Jalen, come take a ride with me."

Jerome sent a text back to Diamond to let her know he was on his way.

The men hopped in the car and headed in the schools direction.

Diamond received Jerome's text.

"Jerome is on his way. We have to stay safe until he gets here."

"We need to get out of this gym. We need to stay where people can see us because they won't do anything with people around."

Johnny started walking down the stairs to find Fred and Mike.

"Johnny, we need to stay up here!" Diamond pleaded with her brother. Johnny kept walking and walked out of the gym and right into the hands of the men. As the doors of the gym opened, the men turned to see Johnny standing there.

"Well, well, look who we have here!" JJ said.

The men grabbed hold of Johnny.

"Where is your sister?" Ricky asked.

"I'm not telling you anything!"

"Suit yourself," Ricky said.

Diamond stood on the other side of the door, listening with tears in her eyes.

"Take a walk with us," JJ said.

"No! I'm not going anywhere," Johnny said as some students turned to look when Johnny raised his voice.

J.J raised his shirt to show Johnny his gun. "Now, let's go!"

The men walked Johnny through the halls and out the doors of the school while some student's standing by watching.

Diamond in tears called Jerome.

"Diamond, are you okay?"

Diamond cried, "They took Johnny."

"What!"

"They took my brother."

"Damn, where are you?"

"Inside the gym."

"Stay there I'm coming in."

Minutes later, Jerome and Jalen pulled up to the school. They jumped out and ran toward the front doors of the school, and when they entered, they saw a couple of teachers standing there talking to two police officers. Jerome and Jalen stopped in their tracks. Jerome pulled out his phone and called Diamond.

"Are you still in the gym?"

Diamond's phone vibrated. She saw it was Jerome calling.

"Yes."

Jerome turned his back toward the police officers and the teachers.

"Come to the front doors of the school and act normal, there are two police officers here with two teachers."

Diamond wiped her eyes before walking through the doors

Diamond opened the door and walked out. She felt the stares from some students and the teachers who were talking with the police officers. Diamond focused her attention on Jerome and the guy standing beside him. She wanted to run right into his arms, but she couldn't.

By the time she reached him, the tears fell.

"Baby, don't cry. Just keep it together until we get to the car," Jerome said as he hugged her.

Jerome walked Diamond to the car. Jerome noticed the officers heading in their direction.

"Hurry and get in and don't look now, but the police officers are heading our way."

They got into the car, and Jerome took off just as the police officer called out to them.

"Hey, stop!"

The police officers ran to their car, turned on their siren and chased after Jerome. Five blocks away, Jerome heard the sirens and looked through his rear-view mirror.

"Damn!"

Diamond and Jalen turned around to see the police car behind them.

"Just be cool and let me do the talking."

Jerome sat with his hands placed on the steering wheel as the officers approached the car. One officer walked toward the driver's side while the other one walked toward the passenger side.

"Where are you going in such a hurry?" Officer Smith asked.

"I was unaware that I was in a hurry. I'm just taking my girl home, she's not feeling well.

Officer Smith looked over at Diamond who laid her head back against the headrest pretending to be sick.

Then Officer Lacy looked at Diamond.

"Can you step outside of the car, please, and bring your backpack with you," Officer Lacy asked Diamond.

"What for? I didn't nothing wrong!" Diamond asked with an attitude.

"Step outside of the car!"

"Just do what she says," Jerome told her.

Diamond stepped out of the car, and officer Lacy escorted her to the back of the vehicle.

"Do you have any identification on you?"

Diamond reached into her backpack and pulled out her ID and handed it to the officer. The officer looked at her ID.

"Diamond Jefferson. Are you in any danger?" Officer Lacy stared at Diamond.

"No, and why would I be?"

"We got word that your brother was escorted out of school by some gang members and then we see you leave with some guys. Be honest with me and tell me what's going on?"

Diamond hesitated before speaking; there's nothing going on. When did it become a crime for people to pick someone up from school?"

"Sir, can I ask why you pulled me over?"

"You can, but I don't have to answer you."

"By law, I have a right to know why you pulled me over."

The officer looked at Jerome before walking back to his car. He pulled a bat out of the back seat. He moved toward the back of Jerome's car and bashed the tail light out with his bat.

"This motherfucker!"

"Be cool, man. He wants you to say something out of line," Jalen warned Jerome.

Diamond and Officer Lacy looked at each other.

"Smith, what are you doing?"

Officer Smith's looked at her and smiled.

"Are you going to stand here and let him get away with this?"

"Hold tight," Officer Lacy told Diamond. Lacy walked over to Officer Smith. "Can I have a word with you?"

Officer Smith looked back at her and continued to walk back to the driver's side of the car and leaned inside the car.

"I pulled you over because you have a busted tail light."

"Okay, sir, I'll get it fixed right away," Jerome said sarcastically. After being ignored, Officer Lacy walked back over to Diamond.

"I'm sorry, but I will deal with him later."

"Diamond, are you sure you're okay?"

"Yes, I'm fine."

Officer Lacy reached into her pocket and pulled out a card and handed it to Diamond.

"If you want to talk, just call me. You're free to go." Diamond hesitated for a minute and then walked back to the car. Officer Lacy noticed.

"We're done here, Smith!" Lacy yelled as she walked back to the police car.

Officer Smith looked at Jerome and then at Diamond before heading back to his car.

"What the hell was that all about," Jalen asked.

"That cop was at the apartment building last night. He's dirty as fuck."

"He sure was. You know that Officer handed me a card and told me if I ever wanted to talk to call her."

"Don't trust her either."

"She seemed genuine. You should have seen the look on her face when the Officer busted your tail light out."

Denise Hill
The Window

CHAPTER TEN

Johnny and four of the gang members pulled up inside the garage. The side door opened and more of the gang members walked out. Johnny tried to be brave, but they scared him. He had no idea what was about to go down.

"Get that Lil nigga out the car," JJ said.

Harry pulled Johnny out of the car and leaned him up against the car.

"Why don't y'all be cool? This dude has nothing to do with this. We want that sister of his."

"My sister has done nothing to you guys, so why are you bothering us?" Johnny asked angrily.

JJ hits Johnny on the side of the head in the temple with the butt of the gun, and he fell to the ground.

"See what you did. Help Lil dude up," Wade said.

JJ pulled at Johnny.

"Get up, man; get up!" JJ yelled.

Johnny doesn't move. JJ noticed blood running down the side of his face. He bent down to feel his pulse, but there was none. JJ looked up at Wade.

"This dude is a fucking wimp. I barely hit him, and now this nigga's dead."

"See! This was all uncalled for. Wait until Deon finds out. He strictly told you guys to get the sister."

"We couldn't find the sister, so we took him as leverage," Ricky said.

Wade looked at Ricky. "What the fuck do you know about leverage? You probably can't even spell it."

The gang members laughed.

Jerome pulled off and continued to check his rearview mirror until the police car turned off.

"We need to get my brother."

"When we get back to the house, I will talk with Ron, Jess, and the others so we can come up with a plan to get him back, but first we have to find out where their hangout is."

Jalen said, "I have a buddy that hangs out with a few of the gang members. I can call him to see if he'll tell me where they hang out at."

"Bet."

Jerome was busy talking to Diamond that he never noticed the police car tailing behind him.

Officer Smith had turned the corner and took a quicker way to get to the interstate and caught up with Jerome once he exited the interstate.

As Jerome pulled into the driveway, the police car stopped and watched as Jerome punched in the code and drove around back.

"Smith! What are we doing here and why are we following them? What is it with you and the driver and why did you break his tail light? When we get back to the station, I'm reporting you!"

"Mind your business, Lacy! So when did partners start telling on each other? What I do should be between the two of us."

"You're dirty, just like everyone said. Take me back to the station, now!"

Officer Smith looked over at Lacy and smiled.

Lacy didn't trust him. She was not happy when she learned she would be work with him.

The day Lacy met Officer Smith

Inside the roll call room, Lt. James walked over to officer Lacy.

"Hey Lacy, come with me; there's someone I like for you to meet."

Lacy followed behind Lt. James as he approached Officer Smith.

"Say hello to your new partner."

The disappointment showed in her face.

"Don't look so disappointed. I know you probably heard a lot of bad things about me, but trust me, none of them are true," Officer Smith said as he laughed.

On the ride to the station, Lacy continued to study Officer Smith. She remembered him having a conversation with a group of men the night at the apartment.

Diamond walked through the door and down the hall to the family room and immediately, Gina knew something was wrong.

"Where's Johnny?"

Gina moved to the entryway to the door and walked down the hall looking for Johnny. Fear written all over her face as she walked back.

"Mom, they took him from school," Diamond cried.

"What!" Gina grabbed her chest. "Who took him and why didn't you help him?"

"Mom, I tried to stop him from leaving the gym where we were hiding until Jerome got there, but he wouldn't listen. Soon as he opened the door of the gym, they were right there."

Ronnie, Jess and the other men were hanging out downstairs when they heard Diamond and Gina cry. The men looked at each other and shot upstairs and ran into the family room. Ronnie got there first. He saw Tonya and Diamond, but he didn't see Johnny.

"Where's Johnny?"

"They took my baby!"

"Some Warlords came to the school and got him," Jerome said.

Ronnie ran his hand through his hair. "See, I told you I didn't trust that nigga Deon." Ronnie walked over to Gina and pulled her to his chest. Ronnie rubbed Gina's back, 'Calm down. We will get him and bring him back, I promise."

Jalen got off the phone, "I think I know where they may have taken him."

All eyes were on Jalen.

"Where?" Ronnie asked.

"A buddy of mine said they hang out at a house on the corner of 34th and Station. He said it's heavily guarded though."

"Let's pack and take a ride," Jerome said.

In the meantime, Gina was sitting in the family room with Tonya holding her close to her chest, rocking back and forth as she shed tears.

Diamond was upstairs in her bedroom, sitting on her bed thinking when she pulled out the card officer Lacy handed her. She debated whether to call her. Diamond dialed the number on the card. It rang three times before Diamond hanged up.

Denise Hill
The Window

CHAPTER ELEVEN

Lacy stepped out of the shower, grabbed a towel, and wrapped it around her body. She moved to the mirror and wiped away the steam with her hand. She examined the bruise on the side of her face carefully. Lacy thought about the ride back to the station. Officer Smith pulled up to an abandoned warehouse and cut the engine.

Lacy turned to look at Officer Smith, "What are we doing here?"

Officer Smith got out of the car and walked around to the passenger side of the vehicle.

"Get out."

Lacy looked at him sideways.

"Get out!" Officer Smith yelled again.

Officer Smith opened the door.

"What?"

"I said get out!"

"I heard what you said, but what I don't understand is why we are here?"

Officer Smith yanked Lacy out and threw her up against the car. Lacy shoved Officer Smith away from her.

"What the fuck is wrong with you?"

"I am so tired of your damn mouth. Why can't you just roll with me?"

"Because I'm not like you. You are dirty as fuck!"

Smith hit Lacy in the jaw with his fist; she stumbled, but caught herself before she fell. Lacy reached for her gun and pulled it out.

"You son of a bitch, if you ever lay another hand on me again, I will make sure I bury your monkey ass six feet under."

"Oh, so you have some balls?" Officer Smith said as he laughed.

"I have more balls than you will ever have you bitch ass nigga."

Lacy backed away from the car. She had no idea where she was, so she pulled her phone out and started walking. She dialed Lt. James.

Officer Smith hopped in the car and followed alongside Lacy.

"Lacy, get in. I'm sorry! I will drive you back to the station; just get in."

Officer Smith pleaded with Lacy several times before Lacy got in the car. She ended her call to the Lieutenant as she got in the car. The two rode back to the station in silence.

Officer Smith pulled into the parking lot and parked. Lacy hopped out and hurried inside. Inside the precinct, Lt. James called out to her.

"Lacy, did you call me?"

Lacy turned around and then looked back at Officer Smith.

"Yeah, I did, but it was by accident."

Lacy turned back around and continued to walk until she came to her locker. Just then her boyfriend Detective Johnson walked up, and he noticed the bruise on her face. He turned her face around so he could get a better look at it.

"Hey, babe, what happened to your face?"

Lacy thought before answering. She noticed Officer Smith as he leaned against the wall directly across from her with a wicked smile on his face.

"I slipped getting out of the car and hit my face against the edge of the door."

Detective Johnson stood there looking at Lacy when he noticed Lacy looking straight ahead, so he turned to see what she was looking at when he saw officer Smith. Johnson looked back at Lacy, who looked upset.

"Did he do this to you?"

Detective Johnson knew all about Officer Smith and was against Lacy partnering up with him.

Lacy turned around, pulled her purse out of the locker, and shut it.

"Answer me, Lacy!"

"No, babe, I told you what happened," Lacy kissed detective Johnson on the lips.

"Are you coming by tonight?"

"Yeah, but it will be after 9."

"Okay, I will see you then."

Lacy walked off. Detective Johnson turned to look at Officer Smith, who was staring back at him with a smile on his face.

"Asshole!" Detective Johnson said under his breath.

Lacy walked out of the bathroom with a towel wrapped around her. She walked down the hall into the kitchen. She opened the refrigerator, grabbed a bottle of water, and walked back down the hall to her bedroom.

Lacy checked her phone and saw a missed call. She looked at the number and didn't recognize it. She checked to see if the caller left a message. When she saw there was no message, she dialed the number back.

Diamonds sat with the phone in her hand when it rang. She saw Lacy's number come across. Diamond answered the phone, but said nothing.

Lacy listened, she heard nothing but breathing on the other end of the phone.

"Diamond, is that you? Are you okay?"

"I need your help," Diamond cried.

"Diamond, where are you? Are you okay?"

"Yes, I'm okay, but my brother."

There was a pause.

"Members of the Warlord gang took my brother. They took him from school."

"Oh, my God! Why didn't you tell me this earlier?"

"Because your partner is dirty, and besides, he knows them."

Lacy put two and two together.

"Diamond, where are you?"

Just then, Diamond remembered what Jerome said about not trusting Lacy. Diamond hung up the phone and cut it off.

Denise Hill
The Window

66

CHAPTER TWELVE

Ronnie and his boys sat in two cars parked four houses down from the gang's house. As they were scoping out the scene, they saw Officer Smith pull up to the house. He got out of his car and walked up the driveway to where Wade and some members were standing.

"What'd up, boy?" Wade said as he embraced Officer Smith.

"Hey, what's going on and where is the boy at?"
Wade looked over at J.J and Ricky.

"Tell him what happened," Wade said.
JJ and Ricky looked at each other.

"The little nigga is dead."

"What the fuck! How did this happen?"

"I guess when I hit him, I hit him a little too hard," JJ said as he looked away.
Officer Smith grabbed JJ By the throat.

"What did I tell you to do, huh? I told you to get the sister and what did you do, you grabbed the brother and killed him. I should lock your little ass up right now."
Jerome sat in the first car with the windows rolled down and by what he was witnessing he knew something had gone wrong.

"He's pissed off about something. Man, I hope what I am thinking hasn't happened."

"I know. Looks like someone fucked up. Are you thinking what I'm thinking?" Jess asked.

"About Johnny?"
"Yeah," Jess said.

"I hope they didn't kill that little dude," Jerome said, sitting in the back seat as he shook his head.

"What did you do with the body?" Officer Smith asked.

"We have done nothing yet, we are waiting until it gets dark and then we will dump his body in the back of the apartments where they lived in the wooded area," Wade said.

"That's a good idea, just make sure there are no witnesses and if there are, well, you know what to do," Officer Smith told Wade. "I'll holler back at you later on tonight."
Officer Smith was walking back to his car when he spotted the two vehicles that he hadn't noticed before. Officer Smith turned on the

ignition, put the car in drive and slowly drove toward the cars. As he did the men in the two vehicles turned their head so he couldn't see their face.

Jalen sat in the first car with Ronnie, Jess, and Jerome. He called his buddy that had given him the address.

"Any news on the young boy?"

"Man, you don't even want to know."

"Tell me it isn't so?"

"I wish I could. Check the wooded area late tonight behind the apartments where he lived. They will dump his body. But you didn't hear this from me."

"Aiight, thanks, man."

"What's the word?" Ronnie asked as he looked back at Jalen through the rearview mirror.

Jalen hesitated, "He's dead. They are planning to dump his body tonight behind the wooded area behind the apartments where they live."

Everyone in the car put their head down.

"Man, this is fucked up!" Ronnie said as he punched the steering wheel with his fist.

Just then Ronnie opened the car door, "What are you doing?" The men asked.

"We can't just waltz up in there like this," Jess tried to convince Ronnie. "Let's go back to the crib and think of a plan to get these assholes."

Ronnie thought about what they were saying and shut the door. He started the car and drove off. The second car followed, not knowing what had happened.

"This is not right," Ronnie repeated. "How could they do him like this? I can't tell his mother?"

"I know, think about how Diamond will feel. She will blame herself, and Gina will too," Jerome said.

Gina heard the back door open. She got up and ran into the hallway as the men walked through the door. She stood until everyone walked through.

Her heart was beating a mile a minute, "Where is he?" Ronnie told her what happened when someone busted through the back door. All heads turned as they drew their and weapons.

"Oh my God!" Gina screamed!

Later that night, Lacy was in the kitchen warming up some carry out food from Panda Express while waiting for detective Johnson to arrive. She couldn't wait for him to come and talk to him about Diamond, her brother, and Officer Smith. She was so ready to take down Officer Smith and anyone else involved. This would mean a promotion to detective for her, and it would take another lousy cop off the streets.

Minutes later, Detective Johnson let himself into Lacy's apartment. He allowed his nose to lead him to the kitchen where Lacy stood in some sexy lingerie. Johnson stood in the entryway admiring her.

"Damn, the food smells good, and you're looking good. What did I do to deserve all this right here?" He said as he made his way further into the kitchen. He grabbed Lacy from behind and pulled her close to him.

"Hey babe, how was your day?"

"Hectic as usual. We busted a couple of gang members on the corner selling."

"What gang?" Lacy eyes lit up.

"Right now I don't want to talk about work. I want to be fed with some food and some love."

Lacy turned around to face him. She looked up and kissed him under his chin. He looked down at her and ran his finger down the side of her face and stopped when he came to her bruise.

"You know we will talk about this, right?"

"We will talk about a lot of things tonight. So let me feed you so we can talk."

Back at the house, Wade was getting ready to take Johnny's body and dump it.

"Man, stop playing and bring little dude here!" Wade yelled as he stood by the trunk of the car ready to put the body in the trunk.

"I'm not playing, he's not here," JJ said.

"So what did he do, get up and walk away?"

"If you don't believe us, why don't you come and look," Ricky said agitatedly.

Wade walked back to where the body was supposed to be. He looked around and then he looked at JJ, Harry and then Ricky.

"So where did he go?"

"Now, that's the one hundred thousand dollar question," Harry said sarcastically.

"I've had just about enough of you," Wade said as he moved to slap Harry, but just then Deon walked in.

"Hey, what's going on here?"

"Your helpers just lost a dead body."

"We did nothing so don't go trying to blame that shit on us," JJ said.

"What dead body?" Deon asked.

"Oh, that's right; I forgot to tell you JJ killed the brother."

"Didn't I tell you to bring me the sister, and that I didn't want any murders on our hands behind this situation? You little Negros just keep fucking shit up for us!" Deon tried to hold his cool.

"You guys go on inside, I want to speak with Wade alone."

The boys went inside, but they didn't stay too far from the door. They wanted to hear what Deon had to say.

"Shhh, be quiet," JJ said.

Outside in the garage, Deon and Wade moved to the other side of the room.

"You know what to do. They will draw too much heat. I want you to take them for a ride."

JJ jumped back when he heard this.

"Hey, where's Sabrina?"

"I don't know why?"

"We need for her to take us somewhere and fast. They are planning on killing us."

"Oh, shit!"

They searched the house for Sabrina, but she was nowhere in sight.

"We have to get out of here and now."

The young men ran out the back door, hopped the fence and ran as fast as they could down the alley.

"I know where we can go; let's go to ole girl's apartment since they are not there anymore, no one will come looking for us there, at least no time soon," Harry said.

"Sounds like a plan."

Denise Hill
The Window

CHAPTER THIRTEEN

Wade and Deon had just finished talking when they walked into the home.

"JJ," Wade called out to him. Then he called out for Ricky and Harry, and then Lil Moe, but they were nowhere to be found. Just then, Sabrina, Wade and Deon's little sister walked through the door.

"Where the hell have you been?"
She looked at him with an attitude, "Excuse you. The last time I checked you were not my daddy."

"Have you seen the boys?" Deon asked.

"Didn't you guys see me walk through the door? I've been gone for about an hour, but I saw them in the den right before I left, why?"

"I need for them to take a ride with me somewhere," Wade replied. Sabrina knew something would happen behind what she had done, but she knew she had done the right thing.

Three hours before, she was sitting in her bedroom listening to music when her bedroom door opened. She blinked twice to make sure she was not seeing things, and as he stumbled further into her room, she knew it was not her imagination.

"Oh my God! You're alive!" Sabrina shouted.

"Help me please," He said as the blood ran down the side of his face.

"I have got to get you outta here."
Sabrina ran to him, and he wrapped his arm around her shoulder.

"Take me home, please," He pleaded.

"Hold on. I think I hear someone coming. Here, hide in my closet."
She helped him to her closet just as her bedroom door opened.

"Who were you talking to?" JJ asked.

"First of all, you need to knock before opening my door and second, I wasn't talking to anyone, and if I was, it's none of your business."

"Aw, don't be mad at me for killing your boyfriend. I didn't mean to."

"Yeah, right! I know you didn't like him and you probably tried to kill him on purpose because you knew I had a crush on him."

"What do you mean tried? I killed him just like I killed Tyree, and the only thing keeping me from killing your little cheating ass is your brother."

"JJ, I never cheated on you so I wish you would stop saying that and get the fuck out of her, anyway."

"You better watch who you are talking to like that," JJ said as he moved closer to Sabrina and grabbed her by the throat.

Sabrina grabbed his hand with both of her hands and tried to pull his hand from around her throat, but she couldn't. She stood there wrestling with his hand, trying to pull it away from her, and when he saw the tears roll down her face, he removed his hands.

Sabrina yelled for dear life as she cried, "Wade, Wade!"

Wade was there in no time, "What the hell is wrong?"

"Your stupid ass worker was trying to choke me to death."

"Man, I was playing with her. You know I would never hurt her."

"If you ever put your hands on her again, it will be the last time you will breathe on this earth. Do I make myself clear?" Wade asked as he grabbed JJ by the throat.

"I got it," JJ said as he jerked away from Wade and walked out the room.

Wade looked over at Sabrina, "Are you okay?"

"Yeah."

"I told you to leave that nigga alone, anyway."

"I wasn't messing with him. I was in my room, minding my business when he burst in."

"I will handle his ass; just wait and see," Wade said as he walked out.

Sabrina locked her bedroom door and ran over to the closet to find him passed out again.

"Oh my God! Wake up," Sabrina said as she shook him a couple of times.

His eyes slowly opened. "Please take me home."

"I will. I have to get you out of here without no one seeing you."

Sabrina helped him up and walked him over to her bed.

"Here, lay here while I get something to wipe your face." Sabrina rushed into the bathroom in her room and grabbed an extra washcloth and wet it. On her way out, someone knocked at her door.

"Who is it?"

"I need to talk with you for a minute," JJ said on the other side of the door.

"If you don't get away from my door, I will call Wade and make him beat your ass."

"I just wanted to talk; I promise."

"What did I just say?"

Sabrina stood there for a minute until she figured he had left. She walked over to the bed and sat down next to him and gently wiped the blood from alongside his face.

"Are you going to take me home before they come looking for me?"

"Yes, I will let nothing happen to you, I promise. I have to figure a way out. Are you able to walk to the backyard by yourself? I park my car in the back. You will need to get in the back and lay down."

"I can do that."

"It will be hard because people are guarding this place like Fort Knox. We have to make it to the back without being seen. Let me go out and check to see who's in the kitchen. I will be right back."

Sabrina was gone for fifteen minutes, and when she came back into the room, she found him asleep.

"Hey you, we have to go now."

She helped him up and out the door, down the hallway to the kitchen. She opened the patio door, and they walked out back to her car. He hopped in the back and laid down while she got in the front. Just as she started the ignition, JJ ran out and stood in front of the car, "Hey, where are you going?"

"Get out of my fucking way you, idiot."

He didn't budge, so she slowly inched toward him and when he realized she would not stop, he moved out of her way before getting hit.

"You stupid bitch!"

"I don't know what I ever saw in him. So where am I taking you?"

"I don't know the address, but I can tell you how to get there."

An hour later, they were in Muncie, Indiana.

"Am I going the right way?"

"Yeah, turn right at the corner."

"My God! Who lives out here in no-man's-land with these beautiful homes?"

"Just a friend who's helping us."

"Whatever you do, you cannot tell anyone where we are."

"I'm not stupid. If my brother finds out that I helped you escape, that will be my ass."

"Why did you help me, anyway?"

"Because I think you are a nice guy who doesn't deserve what they did to you and besides, I always had a little crush on youm anyway."

"Really, how come I never knew that?"

"Because you were always up in Judy's face. You didn't notice anyone else."

"Oh, I noticed you, I didn't think I had a chance with you. Pull in front of the black Iron Gate. Thank you for your help," He said as he was getting out.

"Hey, wait! Here's my number, call me when this is all over or if you need me for anything." Sabrina said.

"I will and thank you again..."

He stood at the gate and pushed the button for the speaker. He waited for a second and then he pushed it again and no response.

"How am I going to get in," He asked himself.

He looked around as if he was looking for an answer from somewhere. Then he noticed the pillars they didn't seem to be too high, so he decided he would climb over the pillars. The idea sounded easier than it was. It took him several attempts to jump and reach the top part which allowed him to pull himself up, and once he was on top of the pillar, he jumped and landed in the grass. When he landed, he hit the same side of his head causing it to bleed again.

He got up slowly and made his way up the long walkway and to the back of the house. He heard his mother and sister crying as he moved closer to the back door. When he opened the door, he saw the men, their weapons drawn.

"Don't' shoot; it's just me!" He yelled.

"Oh, my God! My baby is home safe and sound. Whoever said God doesn't answer prayers is a liar," His mom said as she ran over and hugged him for dear life. Diamond was right behind her.

Ronnie was so relieved along with the other men.

"Oh my God! What happened to the side of your head, and how did you get here?" His mom asked.

"It's a long story mom."

"Well, I have all night."

Everyone gathered around while Johnny told them the story. Afterward, the men stood quietly.

"So, are we safe here now that Sabrina knows where we are?" Jerome asked. All the men were concerned about this but didn't want to ask the question.

"She's cool. She promised that she would tell no one about this."

"Let's hope not, but just in case we all need to be aware of everything."

"Does this mean we don't have to go back to school?" Johnny asked excitedly.

"I received a call from your principal this evening, and we both agreed that it would be in your best interest if you did not return until things die down. Your teachers will email you your homework, and you can email it back."

"Yes!" Johnny shouted.

Denise Hill
The Window

CHAPTER FOURTEEN

Back at the house, Officer Smith walked through the door.
"Where is Sabrina?
"Why?" Wade asked.
"Just bring her ass in here, and I will let her tell you why."
   "Sabrina, get in here!"
Sabrina had no idea that Officer Smith parked on the side street across from Ronnie's home and had seen her drop Johnny off. Sabrina walked into the room. She knew something was up from the way Wade called her.
   "Why don't you tell your brothers where you were this evening?" Officer Smith said.
   "What are you talking about?"
   "Oh, so you're going to play stupid now?"
   "Are you talking about when I dropped Johnny off?"
She knew she was busted, so she came clean.
   "Bingo!" Detective Smith said.
   "I thought you would try to lie your way out of it."
   "I guess you don't know as much as you think you know about me. I don't have to lie about anything." Sabrina rolled her eyes. She despised him more each day.
   "Now you on the other hand, that's a different story." Deon couldn't help but laugh.
   "You are truly my baby sister, and besides, I wanted the girl anyway, and not the boy. What happened to him should have never happened."
Sabrina cracked a smile and look at detective Smith and walked back into the den.
   "Man, y'all need to do something about her and that mouth."
   "You need to stay in your lane, bro," Wade said.
   "Yeah, let's worry about the issue at hand," Deon commented.
Detective Smith shook his head. He wanted so badly to bust Sabrina in her mouth.
   "What are we going to do about the sister?" Wade asked. "I know she will not keep quiet, seeing that she and Tyree were best friends."

"You guys need to find those boys and take care of them. I want no more loose ends, is that clear?" Deon said as he looked at his brother and then Detective Smith.

"I will take care of the girl while Wade takes care of those knuckleheads." Detective Smith said.

After two rounds of lovemaking, Detective Johnson and Lacy lay wrapped in each other's arms. Detective Johnson looked down at her, "So are you going to tell me what happened to the side of your face?"

"If I tell you, promise me you won't do anything stupid."

"Me, do something stupid?"

"Yes."

Lacy sat up in bed with her back against the headboard. She hesitated in telling Johnson because she knew he was a hot head.

"Okay, Officer Smith drove me to an abandoned building, and once we were there, he told me to get out, but I didn't. So he walked around to my side, opened my door and yanked me out. He grabbed me by the collar of my shirt, and I pushed him back. He then hit me with his fist. He said he was tired of my smart mouth. Johnson was livid. He tried to keep his cool, "He did what! Lacy, you should have told me earlier. I would have beat the living daylights out of his ass."

"I know and that's why I didn't want to tell you, and besides, I want him to think everything is cool so when I take his dirty ass down, he won't even see it coming."

By this time, Johnson is out of the bed, pacing back and forth. "Now I am sorry you told me."

"Jay, I told you, you can't do anything stupid. You promised."

"Yeah, yeah, I know," detective Johnson sighed.

"What do you need me to do to help you take his ass out, I mean down?"

Lacy looked at Johnson sideways, "Okay Jay, I am counting on you to keep your word."

"Yeah, yeah."

"I don't know, but I believe Smith is involved somehow with the shooting of the young man at the gas station and I believe this Diamond girl knows something."

"Why do you say that?"

"When she called me earlier today and said she needed help, but then she told me that my partner was dirty. I don't think she trusts me since he is my partner. She probably believes I'm dirty."

"How did she get your number?"

Lacy told Johnson what had transpired earlier that day.

"Okay, she was probably afraid to tell you that the men took her brother because of Smith being there."

"Exactly. I have to get her to trust me and to tell me what she knows about the shooting and Smith."

Later that night, Diamond lay in bed with Jerome making love.

"Diamond! My God!" Jerome yelled out.

"You need to stop making so much noise," she said as she collapsed on top of him.

Jerome laughed.

"I can't help it. You feel so damn good."

"Man, I can't get enough of you." Diamond said as she tried to catch her breath.

"That's good. Now I don't have to worry about you cheating on me."

"Now, I don't know about all that," she laughed as she teased him. Diamond rolled off of Jerome, "You know what? I want to talk with officer Lacy."

"And why would you do that?"

"I was serious when I said I want the people responsible for Tyree's death to pay, and besides, they will try to kill me anyway so I can't tell on them. I have to get them behind bars before they harm my family or me."

"I understand, but do you think you can really trust her?"

"I feel that I can."

"Why don't you set up a meeting with her and I can sneak you out again, but this time we have to stay out of the view of the camera. Ronnie saw us on camera the last time we left the house."

"Do you think he told my mom?"

"Naw, he didn't. He's cool like that."

Denise Hill
The Window

CHAPTER FIFTEEN

The next morning Lacy walked in, and the first person she saw was Smith, who stood there talking to Lt. James. Lacy walked passed and said good morning, more so to Lt. James.

"Good morning."

"Good morning, Lacy," Smith said with a smirk on his face. Lacy looked over at him and rolled her eyes. Lt. James picked up on the tension.

"Good morning, Lacy. Hey, what happened to your face?"

Just then, Johnson walked in and gave Smith the dirtiest look.

"I had an accident yesterday; ain't that right officer Smith?"

"Keep your cool," Johnson whispered into her ear.

Lacy rolled her eyes again and walked to her locker.

Lt. James glared at Smith, "What was that about?"

Officer Smith shrugged his shoulders. Lt. James knew him too well.

"In my office, Smith!"

Inside his office, Lt. James shut the blinds and locked his door. "Now what the hell is going on? I told you when I brought you here that I wanted you to keep your hands clean. "Don't let me find out you're abusing your partner, because I will not lose my job behind you. If anyone finds out that you are my son, I am done. I thought by you not having my last name everything would be cool, but you have to stay on the straight and narrow, especially with Lacy because her boyfriend knows people high up. Do I make myself clear?"

"Yes, pops."

"So what's the issue?"

"The Warlords."

"The Warlords, can't Deon and Wade handle the situation?'

"One of their members killed the young man at the gas station, and there's an eyewitness."

"Can't they make the eye witness disappear, like usual?"

"I told them I would take care of this, but Lacy is putting her nose where it doesn't belong, so I had to teach her a lesson. She tried to disrespect me in front of some dealers and you know I can't have that."

"Yeah, Lacy can be a little mouthy, but just be careful with her."

In the next room, Lacy and Johnson stood by the wall and listened with their ear up against the wall.

"That's it. I don't want you going anywhere with Smith. I will request a new partner for you."

"No, wait," Lacy said as she grabbed hold of Johnson's arm.

"How will I be able to find out what Smith is up to if I can't ride with him anymore? I have to act like nothing's up. I tell you what, I'll wear a wire so we can record everything and you can get me that pin you have so I can videotape him."

"I don't know Lacy, I never want to put you in any danger, and this could get ugly."

"I know, but I want to take his ass down along with his pops if he is involved."

"Let's set up a meeting with some buddies of mine in internal affairs and go from there.

"Sounds like a plan."

"Lacy, please be careful."

"I will."

"Hey, I will give you a phone that has a tracker on it, so I will know where you are at all times. Come on, follow me."

Later that morning, Lacy and Smith were riding around when she received a call from Diamond.

"Hey, is everything okay?"

"Yes, everything is fine," Diamond said. I want to meet up with you and talk to you, alone," Diamond said.

"Sure, when's a good time?" Lacy asked.

"When's a good time for you? Diamond asked.

"Um, I can be there at two," Lacy said as he eyed Smith, who was listening closely to the conversation.

"Where?" Lacy asked, not wanting to say too much.
Diamond told her where and Lacy agreed to meet her.

"Please, make sure you come alone," Diamond said.

"You got it."
Diamond walked into Jerome's room and walked over to him and pulled him close to her and kissed him on the lips.

"It's done. We will meet at 2 pm at Starbucks on East 96th street. I can ask Johnny to watch Tonya for a few hours for me."

"Will Tonya tell your mom you left the house?"

"She won't know I'm gone. I will tell Johnny not to tell her."

"Okay, cool."

At 1 o'clock, Lacy asked Smith to drop her off at the station.

"What are you going to do on your lunch hour?" Smith asked.

"I have a few errands to run."

Smith had a feeling something was up with Lacy, so he lay back after dropping her off.

Lacy went inside the station to find Johnson to let him know what was up.

"Lacy, be careful," He said before kissing her on the lips.

Lacy walked outside and got into her car. Smith parked across from the station and watched. He followed her. He stayed his distance, not to be detected.

He continued to follow her as she pulled into the parking lot of Starbucks and watched her park and was getting ready to leave when he seen Diamond and Jerome get out of their car and met up with Lacy.

"Diamond, I'm so glad you called me," Lacy said as they walked inside.

"That sneaky bitch!" Smith yelled.

Smith wanted to go inside, but decided against it.

Inside, Lacy, Jerome and Diamond sat in the back in the corner."

"Thank you, Diamond, so much for meeting with me. I know you probably are a little hesitant to talk to me, but trust me, I am nothing like Officer Smith. I know he is dirty."

"So why is someone like that still on the force?" Diamond asked.

"Trust me; his days are numbered."

"Diamond, do those men still have your brother?"

"No, he's home, thank God. They thought they had killed him, but they knocked him unconscious, and when he came to, some female helped him and brought him home. They wanted me, but they could not find me, so they took him instead."

"Good. I am glad he is home safe. Now tell me, why were they looking for you?"

"I witness a gang member shoot and kill my best friend. I watched through my telescope as the guy shot Tyree in the head over at the gas station across from our apartment.

"How did they know you saw them? Did you tell anyone?"

"When they shot him, I screamed, and that's when they looked up and saw someone. They had no clue who was looking until they searched our apartment and found the telescope. They found a picture of my family and I, so that's how they knew it was me. I talked with Tyree's family and told them who did it, but I don't know the person's name; I know he's a member of the Warlord gang."

"So you would recognize him if I showed you a picture of him?"
"Yes."
"Can you come down to the station and look at some photos?"
"Do you think that's wise seeing that Officer Smith could be there?" Jerome asked.
"Well, I could bring some photos for you to look at. We can meet here again tomorrow at the same time if that's okay?"
Diamond looked over at Jerome.
"That's up to you?"
"Sure, we can do that."
"Okay, then it's settled. I will bring some photos tomorrow, but if you think of anything else, call me. Oh, and thank you again for meeting me."
"You're welcome."
As they were heading to the door, Diamond sees Officer Smith sitting on the hood of his car.
"Oh my God! There's Officer Smith."
Lacy looked up, "he must have followed me here."
"You guys stay inside until he leaves. Diamond I will call you when the coast is clear."
"Okay."
"If he followed you here, then he had to see us walk inside with you."
"Yeah, you're right."
"He's heading this way!" Diamond yelled frantically.
Lacy looked around for another exit, "Hey, you guys sit back down. I will cut him off, so he doesn't come inside. I will call you once he leaves."
Jerome and Diamond walk back to take a seat. Lacy walked outside before Smith could get inside.
"What are you doing here?"
"I think I should be ask you that question."
"And why is that? I am on my lunch hour."

"Why were you here with Diamond?"

"What, what are you talking about?" Lacy said as she started walking to her car with Smith on her heels.

"Don't play dumb with me."

"I'm not playing dumb. If Diamond was here, it doesn't mean I was having a meeting with her; it just means we were at the same place at the same time."

"Okay, do I look like Boo-boo the fool?"

"Whatever you say, Boo-boo." Lacy laughed and got into her car. She sat there and waited until Smith drove off. Lacy texted Diamond that the coast was clear and she also gave Detective Johnson's name and number and told her that if she didn't hear from her tomorrow to call Johnson. Lacy had a bad feeling that something was about to go down.

Denise Hill
The Window

CHAPTER SIXTEEN

When Lacy got back to the precinct, she found Johnson talking to Lt. James. She took a seat at a desk, waiting for him to finish up. Lacy turned around and found Smith standing there watching the men talk. She continued to have this feeling in her gut that something was about to go down, but she couldn't figure out what. Smith pulled up a chair right next to her, "So are you going to tell me what your meeting with Diamond was about?"

"Why do you insist that I was meeting with Diamond? I told you I went there to have lunch, and that's it. What I want to know is why did you follow me there?"

"I didn't follow you just like you didn't meet with Diamond."
Lacy looked at Smith and rolled her eyes. "Don't you have anything to do?"

"Yes, I do, but I can't do it without my partner."

"Ugh, you can be such a pest sometimes."
Smith laughed, "Come on lunchtime is over."
Lacy got up and motioned for Johnson to call her.
Smith and Lacy patrolled several areas in silence until they got a call about a robbery in progress.

"A robbery in progress at 1601 North College Avenue at Community Spirits liquor store, two black male assailants armed and dangerous," the dispatcher said.
Smith turned on his siren and headed in that direction. It took him ten minutes to get there, and by the time they got there, other officers were on the scene. There was yellow tape blocking the front of the store.
Smith and Lacy got out of the car and made their way in front of the store. Smith raised the yellow tape and went under it while Lacy scanned the area and saw Johnson. She made her way over to talk with him.

"Hey babe, what happened here?"

"Two young thugs robbed and killed two of the workers. A female in her early 30s and a male in his late 40s, both African Americans. When is this shit going to stop?"

"I know, I feel so helpless right now."

Smith stood back in the doorway and watched Lacy and Johnson.

"Hey, I met with Diamond today, and she said she could identify the guy who shot her best friend. So I'm planning on bringing her some photos to look at tomorrow, but I'm a little worried because Smith followed me there and saw us. Now he keeps asking me why I was meeting with her."

"What did you tell him?"

"I told him I didn't meet with her, but I know he knows I'm lying."

"I tell you what, I will follow you tomorrow to your meeting with her. I talked to a friend in internal affairs, and he wants to set up a meeting with us next week, but in the meantime, he has sent a request to Lt. James to partner you up with someone else. That's what I was talking to Lt. James about when you walked in. He wanted to know if I had something to do with the request, and I told him no. He may ask you the same thing. Next week you will have a new partner."

"Thanks, babe, I owe you."

"Yes, you do, and I plan to collect on it."

Jerome pulled into the driveway and drove around back. He put the car in park and cut the engine.

"Remember, give me time to go down to the security room and shut the backyard camera off."

"Okay, just text me once you have shut it off."
A minute later, Diamond gets the text message that the coast was clear. She made her way inside and acted as nothing had happened.

"Where were you," Tonya asked as Diamond walked into the family room.

"I was downstairs. Where were you?" Diamond asked as she touched Tonya's nose with the tip of her finger.
Tonya laughed, "I was in here watching cartoons."

"Are you hungry?"

"Yes."

"What do you want to eat?"

"Pizza."

"That figures. Don't you get tired of eating pizza?"

"How about I how go get some burgers, fries, and milkshakes for us?" Jerome asked.

"That sounds much better," Johnny said.

"Okay," Tonya said.

"Make me a list of what you guys want while I run to the bathroom."

Later that evening, as Lacy stepped out of the shower, she heard movement in the living room.

"Is that you, Johnson?" She called out. When she didn't get a response, she wrapped the towel around her and made her way out of the bathroom and down the hall to the living room. She didn't see anyone, so she walked down the hall to her bedroom. As she was drying herself off, she heard a noise again. Lacy slipped on her shirt and a pair of yoga pants and was getting ready to walk out when she came face to face with Smith.

"What the hell are you doing here and how did you get in?"

"That should be the least of your worries."

"What is that supposed to mean?"

Smith bent down and grabbed Lacy's shoes and handed them to her, "Here put these on."

"What for, I'm not going anywhere."

"Lacy, do as I say and put the damn shoes on!"

Lacy did what Smith told her and put her shoes on. Smith pulled out a gun and pointed it at her, "Let's go!"

"Where are we going?"

"We are going for a ride."

"Smith, I hope you know Johnson will be here any minute now."

"Well, he's not here at the moment is he, so let's go!"

"Can I at least grab my jacket?"

"Hurry!"

"Dang, why are you so angry?"

"Because I have had it with you."

"What have I done to you?"

Lacy grabbed her jacket and put it on. She looked at Smith when his phone rang. She grabbed her cell phone, charger, and car keys and put them inside of her jacket, but not before dialing Johnson's number.

Lacy made her way to where Smith stood. She glanced at her gun on her dresser, "Don't you even think about it." Smith said as he pointed his gun at her again. "Okay, let me call right back," Smith said to whoever was on the other end.

Johnson was on his way over to Lacy when he received a call from her, and before he could say anything he heard a male voice, so he just listened. It took him a minute to realize who the male voice belonged to Smith.

"Where are we going Smith?"

"You will see once we get there."

"What if I say I don't want to go?"

"You don't have a choice, and besides, it's for your own protection."

Lacy stopped when they got to the front door, "What do you mean for my own protection?" She was trying to stall until Johnson got there.

"Lacy, move your ass!"

"I'm sorry Smith, but I am not going anywhere with you."

"Lacy, don't make me hurt you!" Smith shouted. "Now getta walking!"

As Lacy made her way outside her door, there were several people in the hallway talking, so Smith puts his gun away and at that very moment, Lacy took off running down the hall to the stairwell. She ran down ten flights of stairs and out the back door to her car and was inside and pulling off when Smith finally made it out the back door. He was struggling to catch his breath.

Lacy pulled onto the street, reached in her pocket to grab her phone. She realized her phone was still on and that Johnson was probably still on the other end.

"Johnson, Johnson, are you there?'

"Yes, I'm here, Lacy. What the hell is going on?"

"Smith broke into my place and held me at gunpoint, but I got away."

"What the fuck! Where are you now?"

"Heading South on Allisonville Road. I'm coming to your place."

"Okay, let me turn around because I was on my way to your place."

"Let yourself in once you get there."

"Oh shit! Smith is right behind me."

"Can you get to Buffalo Wild Wings some from internal affairs are there? I will call and let them know what's going on?"

"Yeah, I can get there."

Johnson hung up from Lacy and called one of his buddies to let him know what was going on and to be on the lookout for Lacy.

Lacy had just pulled into the parking lot of Buffalo Wild Wings when Lance got a call from Officer Smith. Lance was sitting across from the men in internal affairs and excused himself from the table.

"Smith, what are you doing calling me? I told you I would be with my group."

"Lacy is heading inside, so you better make damn sure she says nothing about me breaking into her place and holding her at gunpoint."

"And how am I supposed to do that? There are six other men here."

"You better figure something out because if I go down, so do you!"

"Are you threatening me, Smith?"

"No, that's a promise."

"Man, I have nothing to do with whatever you are doing." Lance shook his head and disconnected the call.

Smith sat outside in the parking lot and waited. He was still there when Johnson showed up.

Smith dialed Deon's number, "Hey man, we need to regroup at the house as soon as possible. Have some of your men there. We have a job to do. I'm heading your way now."

After the call, Deon rounded up the men and waited for Smith to arrive.

CHAPTER SEVENTEEN

Thirty minutes later, the group was sitting around the table when Smith walked in.

"So what's up?" Deon asked.

"We got to take them out tonight," Smith said. "Diamond has been meeting with my partner Lacy. I have no idea what she has told her or what she knows. I can't take a chance on her telling her what she saw that night and everything pointing to us."

"I agree."

"Here's what we will do."

Smith sat down and explained every detail to the guys.

"We will wait until everyone is asleep because there are cameras all around the house."

"And how do you know this?" Wade asked.

"Because I've been scoping the place out. There's a gate, but you have to have the combination. I have something for that, but if that doesn't work, we will have to climb over the Pillars."

"Climb, I don't know about all that," Deon said.

"Well, let's hope I can figure out the combination. And we need to take your SUV's. I don't want to take my car because a cop car in the neighborhood will draw too much attention. We will have to dress in all black. I would hate for the white neighbors to call the cops because they see some niggers in their neighborhood."

Once she was inside Buffalo Wild Wings, Lacy stood in the entryway since she had met none of the men from internal affairs, she had no idea who was who, so she waited or Johnson.

While waiting, she noticed a large man walking toward her, staring at her intensely. She was almost afraid.

Minutes later, Johnson ran inside. Johnson walked Lacy over to the table of men.

"Everyone this is Lacy Cummings. Lacy this is Luther, Jack, Rick, Norman, Roger, and Sam."

"Hey, nice to meet you guys."

"Sorry that we had to meet like this," One man spoke.

"Me too."

"Lacy, why don't you have a seat and fill us in on what's going on with Smith," Norman said.

One man looked around, "Hey, where's Lance?"

"He was on the phone, and then I saw him walk out," Luther said.

It dawned on Lacy that was probably the person she had seen leaving.

"Can I trust him?" Lacy asked.

"Just as much as we can," Jack laughed.

"Jack, all jokes aside, let's get down to business." Johnson said

Lacy and Johnson filled everyone in on what happened.

"And he held you at gunpoint?" Luther asked.

"I say we bring his ass in."

"No Jack, we can't bring him in; if we do, we can never get everyone involved."

"I agree with her," Johnson said.

"So, do we know where the family is?" Jack asked.

Lacy was a little hesitant to answer.

"Babe, you can trust these guys. I trust them with my life."

"Okay, if you say so, yes, I know where they are."

"We need to have two officers sit outside the home just in case Smith and his buddies try something."

"That sounds like a good idea," Johnson said.

"I don't know." Lacy was unsure if this would make things worse.

"Okay, well what about some unmarked cars? Would that make you feel any better?"

"Let us think about it overnight. In the meantime, I will take Lacy home with me, and we will meet first thing in the morning to figure out what to do about the family and about Smith."

"Okay, that sounds like a plan," Norman said

"Damn, where the hell is Lance?" Jack asked.

Jerome and Diamond lay in each other's arms, kissing, "Man, I could go another round."

"I bet you could."

"When this mess is over, I want us to move in together. We can get us a place."

"But I want to go to college."

"That's cool. What college do you want to go to?"

"Michigan State University."

"Well, we can wait until after you graduate, that will give me more time to have everything together the way I want it."

"By the time I graduate, you probably won't even be thinking about me."

"And why do you say that?"

"Jerome, you could have any woman you want, why me?"

"Diamond you're different, you don't want me for what I can do for you. You have never asked me for anything, and that's why I want to give you everything."

"Jerome, you're so sweet and thoughtful."

"Look, I want to show you something." Jerome walked over to his closet opened it and pulled out a black duffle bag. "You see this bag here; if anything should ever happen to me, I want you to take this bag with you and never let it out of your sight. I want you to call this man here and tell him what has happened. Keep this card with you at all times. I don't want to scare you, but we have no idea what will go down."

"Jerome, baby, nothing will happen to you. We are safe here. No one can get in here."

Jerome knew better, "Diamond, just remember what I said."

"I will. See, I just took a picture of the card so it will be on my phone. Are you satisfied?"

"Yes, now bring your pretty little self here."

"Let me take a quick shower first."

Diamond put the card in the side compartment of the duffle bag before heading to the bathroom.

CHAPTER EIGHTEEN

Midnight, four men emerged from a black Envoy, and four from a Jeep Cherokee dressed in black.

They parked on the side street a block away from the house. Smith was aware of the security cameras outside the home, and that's why he waited until midnight and made sure everyone wore black. The men stood in front of the home outside the gate. Smith pulled out a piece of tape and pressed it against the keypad. He pulled a tool out that looked like a makeup brush, brushed some black powder against the clear tape, and blew it off. Once Smith blew it off, he could see the fingerprints. He placed the tape onto a white piece of paper and held the paper next to the keypad. The fingerprints showed the following numbers 6541. Now he had to figure out the order. He tried using the numbers on the paper several times. He tried numbers 1654, and that didn't work. He then tried 5164, 1645, 6145, and 6541.

"Come on, Smith. I could have climbed over by now," one of the young men said.

"Hold your damn horses." Smith looked up and said.

Smith tried another number, but that didn't work. Then he tried 4516, and to his surprise, the gate opened.

"That's what I'm talking about," Wade said.

As the gate opened, the men walked up the walkway, and when they got halfway up, one of the security lights turned on, and it buzzed inside the home.

Inside the home

Ronnie was the first one to wake up. He jumped up and grabbed his phone and check the outside of his house and when he saw the gate open and he knew something was up.

Ronnie ran downstairs to the security room, but Jerome had already beaten him there, and then the other men ran in.

"What the hell is going on?" Jess asked.

"I believe we have some visitors," Ronnie answered.

Ronnie opened the cabinet to the guns and ammunition.

Every man grabbed a weapon and some ammunition.

Outside the house, three men tossed gasoline onto the house, the cars, and the lawn. One man shot out three lights and cameras in the front, and the other men ran around back and did the same.

Minutes later a loud boom was heard with inside the house. Ronnie ran upstairs first. They shot him at close range in the head. Jess came running out after Ronnie and got a shot off, but not before taking a bullet to the chest. Jalen, Donnie, and Leon came out blasting. They killed three men and then a fourth one.

Gina heard the loud sounds of gunshots and ran into Diamond's room to find Tonya in bed and Diamond missing. Johnny ran downstairs to see what was going on and when he realized what was happening, he turned to run, but they hit him in the forehead by a bullet.

Gina grabbed Tonya and ran downstairs to look for Diamond when she saw her son lying in a puddle of blood.

"Oh my God! No!" Gina screamed as she bent down and grabbed Johnny's dead body.

Jerome runs upstairs and runs into his room and in the bathroom.

Diamond had just stepped out the shower when she ran into Jerome.

"What is it?"

Then they heard sounds of a machine gun going off.

"Oh my God!" Diamond screamed.

"Stay here," Jerome ran and got the duffle bag. "Remember what I told you?"

"Yes," Diamond said as the tears ran down her face.

"Stay in here and keep this door shut. I'll be right back."

"No, please don't leave me."

Jerome kissed her and looked into her eyes, "I'll be right back, I promise."

"No, Jerome," Diamond yelled as he shut the bathroom door.

He stood on the other side of the door for a minute before heading toward his bedroom door. Jerome stood there listening to the screams and the gunshots and when they all stopped. He slowly opened the door and stuck his head out. Once he saw the coast was clear, he walked out to the hallway covered with bodies. He fell back against the wall in disbelief, "Oh my God!" Just then Officer Smith stood there laughing, "I see we meet again," Smith said before shooting Jerome in the shoulder and then in the leg. Jerome's body fell to the ground.

Diamond slowly opened the bathroom door. She listened for any sounds of movement and when she heard nothing she ran and grabbed her cell phone and ran back into the bathroom.

Diamond nervously dialed Officer Lacy's number.

Lacy snuggled up with Johnson when she heard her phone on the fourth ring. She looked at the clock on the nightstand before grabbing her phone. When she saw it was Diamond calling, she answered quickly.

"Diamond, is everything okay?"

Diamond whispered, "No, there are people here, and they are shooting." Just then Diamond heard the bathroom knob turning. She tiptoed into the shower and disconnected the call.

Smith was just about to open the bathroom door when one of his men yelled out to him.

"Smith, let's get out of here, the house is in flames."

Diamond's heart dropped to her stomach. She had to get to her family and get them out of there. She waited a few minutes to make sure the coast was clear and then she slid on her sweatpants, hoodie and shoes. She grabbed the duffle bag and made her way to the bedroom door. She cracked the door opened and was getting ready to walk out when she heard her cell phone ringing, but then she heard Jerome," Diamond, get out of here, the house is on fire." Then he passed out.

Diamond looked up, and when she did, she saw her mother, her brother, and her sister. She ran to them screaming, "No, No, please God, no!"

She ran to her mother first, dropped to her knees, and tried to wake her. Then she looked over at her brother, and saw the bullet hole in his forehead, and then Tonya. Her poor sister had no idea what hit her. She received a bullet to the chest.

Diamond sat there on the floor as the fire consumed the house holding her mother's head in her lap crying. The smoke burned her eyes as the tears rolled down her face. She coughed as she inhaled the smoke.

Diamond looked over at Jerome and saw him move. She laid her mom's head down softly on the floor and crawled over to Jerome, who coughed.

"Oh my God, Jerome, you're alive. I got to get you out of here."

Diamond helped Jerome stand. She put his arm around her neck and grabbed him by the waist. They moved toward the back door.

"Don't forget the duffle bag," Jerome whispered as he continued to cough.

Diamond reached down and grabbed hold of the bag as they moved closer to the door.

"It's too much fire, we can't make it," Diamond said. "I will have to break the patio glass."

"It's still too much fire," Jerome said.

"Fire or not, we are going through this motherfucker."

Diamond ran into the kitchen and grabbed a kitchen chair. She ran to the patio glass door, took two steps backward and reared back, and threw the chair, shattering the glass. She grabbed the duffle bag and threw it through the fire. She looked at Jerome, "We got to do this, babe."

"Baby, I can't make it go without me," Jerome said as he fell to his knees.

"No, I can't lose you too. You're all I got, so get your ass up."

Diamond pulled Jerome through the fire, and as she pulled him out, his shirt caught fire. Diamond continued to pull him until they were away from the fire. Diamond hit his arm, trying to put the fire out with the duffle bag. Once the fire was out, Diamond heard voices coming near, "Oh my God, it's Officer Smith and two of his buddies."

"Run Diamond, I can't make it."

"No, I can't leave you."

"There's no need for both of us to die. Now go!" He shouted.

Diamond kissed him on the lips and grabbed the bag. She started running, and then she stopped and turned around, and when she did, she saw Smith standing over Jerome.

"Say Goodnight bitch," Smith said before firing a shot into Jerome's chest.

Diamond took off running and stopped when she came to the fence. There was no way out; he trapped her. She turned around to see Smith walking toward her, smiling. She stood there frightened.

Smith continued to walk toward her. He stopped three feet from her, and he raised his gun. Diamond closed her eyes. She didn't want to see the bullet coming.

The End of part One

Part Two of
The Window
Coming soon!!!

www.ingramcontent.com/pod-product-compliance
Lightning Source LLC
Chambersburg PA
CBHW080817250626
47159CB00010B/3418